Right Kind of Wrong

The Loves of Lakeside

Right Kind of Wrong

MIMI FRANCIS

4 Horsemen
Publications, Inc.

Dedication

To the bookworms and coffee fanatics. You are my people.

Table of Contents

Chapter 1

Nate

A noticeable energy filled the room, a mixture of anticipation and excitement. Nate approached the table, eyeing the eight-ball perched precariously near the corner pocket and the cue ball in the center of the table. He contemplated his shot, envisioning it in his head.

He leaned over, lined up the pool cue to ensure the correct angle, and took a few practice strokes to gauge exactly how hard he needed to hit the ball for an exact strike. The room fell silent, the only sound the faint hum of the overhead fluorescent lights.

Nate dragged in a deep breath, relaxed his shoulders, and tapped the white ball. It rolled smoothly across the green felt and hit the eight ball, which dropped into the corner pocket with a satisfying thud.

An eruption of cheers and applause exploded around him as he dropped the cue on the table and raised his arms above his head.

"There it is!" he shouted. "Whoo-hoo!" He spun in a circle, laughing at the shocked faces of his competitors.

A chorus of boos echoed back at him. He flipped off the crowd as he headed back to the bar. Why anybody bothered to play pool against him, he'd never know. He couldn't lose.

Nate stepped behind the bar, grabbed a water from the cooler, and chugged it. He did a quick check of the bar to make sure his servers were on the floor and the customers were being helped.

A cute brunette sat on a stool across from him and smiled. He dropped the empty water bottle in the recycling bin and smiled at her as he leaned on the bar.

"Hi, I'm Nate," he said.

"I'm Mary," she said. "That was a great game of pool you played. Do you practice a lot?"

He nodded. "Every day. It's not too difficult when you own the place."

Mary propped her chin on her hand, her grin widening. "Wait? You own this place? Really?"

He smirked. "Yes, really."

"That's cool."

"I've never seen you in here before," Nate said. "Do you go to Lakeside College?"

"Yes. I'm getting my masters in anthropology," she explained. "I got my bachelor's degree from U of M, though."

"So, you're new in town." Nate tapped his fingers on the bar and gave her his best smile. "What can I get you to drink?"

"How about a White Claw? Raspberry?" she replied.

He did his best not to roll his eyes. Why did every girl who came through the door of the Time Out Bar & Grill have to be so cliché?

"Do you have your ID?" he asked.

Mary giggled, took her ID out of her back pocket, and set it in front of him. Nate examined it, looking for the telltale signs of a fake.

She narrowed her eyes and acted offended. "It's real, I promise." She sat up straighter. "I'm twenty-three."

He raised an eyebrow. "Twenty-three, huh?" He squinted at her license and turned it in the light, catching the holographic image in the corner.

"You're right, it is real," he said, holding it out to her.

Mary took it from him, her fingers brushing his. Nate grabbed a White Claw from the cooler, popped it open, and handed it to her.

"So, *Mary*, do you have a boyfriend? Girlfriend? Significant other?"

"I'm single," she said. "How about you?"

"Oddly enough, I am single, too." Nate chuckled. "Why don't you hang out here for a while, and we'll get to know each other?"

"I think that sounds like fun," she replied. "Lots and lots of fun."

———

Nate held Mary's hand loosely in his as they tiptoed through the living room and out the front door. They stepped outside, and he shut the door behind them. Mary shivered and snuggled up to him.

"It's cold," she muttered.

"Because it is October in Montana. It won't be much longer until we have snow." He glanced down at her bare legs and back up. "It's time to put the shorts away."

Mary rolled her eyes. "I like my shorts." She kissed him on the cheek. "Call me later?"

He shrugged. "If I have time."

"Maybe I'll stop by the bar after my class this afternoon. We can have lunch."

Nate shook his head. "We're closed today, so no lunch. Look, you're cold. Go get in your car."

She gave him a funny look before she hurried down the driveway to her car parked on the street. She waved at him as she pulled away from the curb. He raised his hand in a half-assed wave and opened the door.

"New girlfriend?" a voice said behind him.

Nate jumped, smacking his elbow on the doorknob. "Ouch. Damn it, Tasha, don't sneak up on me."

Nate's twin sister, Natasha, put her hands up and giggled. "I wasn't! Sheesh."

"What are you doing up so early?" he asked. He stepped inside and kicked the door closed.

"It's not that early. It's after seven," Natasha replied. "I have a full day at the theater. I assume you are up early because you had to say goodbye to your new girlfriend."

He sighed and rolled his eyes. "She's not my girlfriend. She's a girl I met at the bar last week."

"How long is this one going to last?" Natasha asked.

"I don't know. Not much longer." Nate shrugged. "Why don't you worry about your relationship with Mason and stay out of my business?"

His sister stuck her tongue out at him. "My relationship is fine, thank you. Make me some coffee while I get dressed. Mason will be out soon."

Mason was Nate's best friend, roommate, and Tasha's boyfriend. He had been friends with the Garin twins since they were kids. The three of them grew up together. Mason had been in love with Natasha their whole lives, but it wasn't until recently that the two of them started dating. Nate was thrilled for them.

Even though he was happy that his best friend and his sister were together, seeing his sister walking around in Mason's T-shirts, or watching them hold hands or cuddle, was weird. Worse than any of that, Nate despised hearing the two of them through the thin bedroom walls.

It had gotten so bad; he had to talk to Mason about it. It was the most unbelievably awkward conversation he'd ever had with his best friend. Just thinking about it again made him want to scrub his brain out with bleach.

Nate started a pot of coffee and took a pop tart out of the box in the cupboard. He ripped open the package and ate it while he waited for the coffee to finish.

Mason came into the kitchen, dressed for his morning run in shorts and a zipped-up hoodie. He had his long, black hair pulled into a bun at the back of his head, and his shoes were in his hand. He sat at the table to put them on. "You're up early," he said. "Where are you going?"

Nate talked around a mouthful of pop tart. "Work. We're deep cleaning the bar, so we're shut down for the day. I have the staff coming in to do a deep dive into every nook and cranny. I need to grab some cleaning supplies on my way in, and I wanted to get an early start." He grabbed a cup from the cupboard and tossed it to Mason, who caught it with one hand.

"Hey, you want to go get dinner with us tonight?" Mason asked. "Bring a date." He grinned as he poured coffee into the cup and grabbed sugar packets and creamer. "What's her name this week?"

Nate scowled. "I'm not seeing anybody right now."

"Bullshit," Tasha yelled from the other room. "What's-her-name just left." She came around the corner, dressed in jeans and a sweater, hopped onto the counter, and sat down, her legs swinging. Mason stepped between her legs, slid his arms around her, and kissed her with a loud smack.

"We're not serious," Nate insisted.

"You're never serious," Natasha muttered.

"You took the words out of my mouth, babe." Mason glanced at him. "What's wrong with this one?"

Nate sighed. "Nothing. I don't know. Maybe I'm tired of the dating scene."

Mason snorted. "Or have you finally blown through all the women in Lakeside?"

"Wow, you're hilarious," Nate deadpanned. He grabbed his car keys and phone off the table by the front door. He couldn't stomach another minute with his sister and Mason. "I'll let you know about dinner."

He slammed the door harder than intended and almost dropped his phone, juggling it briefly before securing it, only to have it go off right away. It was a text from Brooke, his assistant manager, making him grunt in frustration. She was running late for work.

It's going to be a long day.

The sound of banging drew Nate's attention to the house next door. His neighbor stood on her front stoop, staring at her door. Her blonde was piled on top of her head in a messy bun, her too-large glasses perched on the end of her nose, and her oversized sweatshirt hung to the middle of her thighs. A backpack sat on the ground by her feet, and she scowled, marring her pretty face.

"Are you okay?" he yelled.

His neighbor jumped and shrank into her sweatshirt. She nodded her head so hard her hair fell out of her bun, the soft curls framing her face.

Nate walked a few feet onto her front lawn. "Are you sure?" he asked.

"Yes, thank you," she replied, pushing her glasses up her nose. She spoke so quietly he barely heard her.

He shrugged, continued across the lawn, and got into his car. He started it, but he didn't leave right away. Instead, he watched as his neighbor pushed open her window and wiggled through it, her shoe falling off and landing in the dirt as she kicked and squirmed. Nate shook his head and chuckled. What the hell was she doing?

It occurred to him that he didn't know her name, and they'd never spoken. She kept to herself and avoided any contact with anyone in the neighborhood. Mason was wrong. He hadn't met and dated *all* the women in Lakeside.

Not yet, anyway.

Chapter 2

Faith

Coffee spilled over the edge of the cup onto Faith's hand, burning it. She cursed under her breath, dropped her backpack on the ground, and put her cup on the window-sill. The front door swung closed behind her while she worked on getting the lid on the cup nice and tight—something she apparently hadn't done earlier. After she double-checked that the lid was actually in place and her coffee wouldn't spill, she picked up her backpack, opened the front pocket, and reached for her keys.

They weren't there.

Faith closed her eyes, and immediately the image of them on the table between two stacks of books popped into her head.

"Dammit," she muttered.

She wiggled the doorknob, knowing it was no use. She always locked it when she walked out the door. Always. She banged her fist against the door.

She jumped when she heard someone yell, "Are you okay?" from across the lawn.

It was one of her neighbors, not that she bothered to look up. She kept her head down and nodded so hard her stupid hair fell out of the loose bun she'd put it in.

"Are you sure?" he asked.

Faith swallowed down her nerves. "Yes, thank you," she called without looking up. She pushed her glasses up her nose.

At first, she wasn't sure he heard her, but after a few seconds, his car door opened and closed.

Thank God.

She didn't have the strength to deal with some guy swooping in to rescue her, and she didn't need anyone else to solve her problems.

The window next to the door was open about an inch, just enough for her to get her fingers in and push it open. It wasn't a big window, but there was room for her to climb through it.

"Okay, here goes nothing," she mumbled under her breath.

Faith shimmied through the window. Her shoe slipped off, but that wasn't a problem. At least she wouldn't be walking around outside without it, since it was on the porch. The pile of books under the window tipped over, and the lamp fell off the table and hit the wall, but she made it inside. Heathcliff stared at her disdainfully from his perch on the kitchen counter. Her cat had no patience for her antics.

Once she had her keys in hand—and her fingers wrapped around them for good measure—she stepped outside, re-locked the door, and grabbed her things, including her shoe. She checked her watch.

Yep, she was definitely going to be late for work.

Sure enough, Faith walked through the front door of the library ten minutes late. Caroline Stover, her boss, and friend, watched her as she stumbled in, set her things behind the desk, and dropped into her chair.

"Rough morning?" Caroline asked.

"I locked my keys in the house and had to climb through the window to get them," she replied, poking at her glasses again. "So, yeah, a little rough."

Caroline snorted and covered her mouth with her hand.

"Don't laugh at me," Faith mumbled.

Caroline shrugged. "I'm sorry, but I'm picturing you wiggling through a window. You're so tall, it must have been a treat."

Her friend was right. She was tall—six feet, to be exact. It had been an issue her whole life and one of the many, many reasons things had been difficult for her as a child.

Faith closed her eyes and smiled. She probably looked like a total klutz and completely ridiculous as she wiggled through her window. A giggle escaped her.

"It wasn't easy." She shook her head. "I can't believe I had to do that."

"You need one of those rock things where you hide your keys," Caroline said.

Faith nodded. "I'll order one from Amazon. Now, can we please stop talking about it and get to work?"

Caroline laughed. "Sure. It's not like there won't be something else to talk about later today."

She rolled her eyes. "As much as I'd like to argue with you, you're probably right."

—

She sat on the floor in the back room surrounded by books, paper cuts on her hands, dust in her hair, and an ache in her neck from looking down for the last two hours.

There was no place she'd rather be.

If someone told her ten years ago she'd be a librarian in a small town in Montana, she'd have laughed at them. Working as a librarian was a dream, but she never thought she'd get there. It required a college education—a master's degree—and when she was younger, she didn't know how she was supposed to get one of those. According to three different foster parents, a counselor at one of the five different high schools she attended, and three of her four case managers, foster kids rarely went to college. Her dream of being a librarian was unlikely to come to fruition. If she hadn't met Professor Hudspeth, she wouldn't be doing what she loved.

"Faith?"

"Back here," she yelled.

Caroline came around the corner. "How's it going?"

She smiled. "Aside from being covered in dust and having about thirty paper cuts, it's going great. I'm almost done sorting the books from the back room. They've been entered into the system. Next up is organizing and tagging the ones we're keeping and donating those we don't want anymore."

"By donating, do you mean 'taking them home?'" Caroline asked.

Faith shook her head and laughed. "It's not my fault one perk of my job is rescuing books that need a home."

"Your place isn't big enough to hold all those books."

She shrugged. "I just need some bookcases."

Caroline rolled her eyes. "There aren't enough bookcases in the world. Anyway, I came up here to see if you were done. It's after six."

Faith pushed her glasses up her nose and squinted at the clock on the wall. "It is? I didn't realize it had gotten so late."

"A few of us are going out for drinks," her boss said. "Would you like to go?"

She shook her head. Caroline asked her this question every Friday. And every week, her answer was the same. "No, but thank you for thinking of me. I have to go home and feed Heathcliff."

Caroline crouched beside her. "You know, you need to get out there and socialize. Make some friends."

"I have friends," she protested.

"You have me," Caroline murmured. "And your cat. You need more people in your life."

Faith must have looked as horrified as she felt, because Caroline smiled gently and squeezed her shoulder.

"Maybe next time."

She waited until Caroline was gone, then she got to her feet and brushed off her hands and jeans. She collected her things from the drawer in her desk and said goodbye to Josie, the evening librarian. Next to the back door was a large bag filled with books they had taken out of circulation. She picked them up, carried them to her car, and put them in the back seat. More books to add to her collection.

Faith didn't need friends. She had books. They were more than enough company.

Chapter 3
Nate

"Nate! Phone! I think it's your girlfriend."

The bar phone clattered on the counter as Brooke dropped it, then she grabbed the bucket of soapy water and headed for the back room.

"Thanks," he muttered after her, though she probably didn't hear him. He propped the phone between his head and shoulder. "Hello?"

"Hey, it's Mary."

He closed his eyes and took a deep breath. Mary wasn't his girlfriend. He never used the word girlfriend when referring to the women he dated; he hadn't used that word since Elle. He might never use it because of her. Besides, he didn't have the energy for a relationship. They were friends, *not* girlfriends. He devoted all of his free time to the Time Out Bar & Grill.

"Hi," he mumbled.

"You didn't answer your phone." Her voice was sharp and biting.

"I don't have it on me," he explained. "I'm *busy*."

"Oh, okay. Well, I thought we could go to a movie tonight or something," Mary said. "Are you free?"

Nate pinched the bridge of his nose. The last few days, he'd gotten the feeling it was time to move on. When the women wanted more—more dates, more commitment, more *anything*—he broke it off. Love was complicated, and he struggled with it more than most people realized. He didn't want or need it screwing up his life again.

"Listen, Mary, we need to talk."

The breakup took less than two minutes; Nate was better at breakups than relationships. He usually stayed friends with the women he broke up with, a necessity when he owned a popular bar in a small college town. He couldn't afford to alienate anyone.

Brooke, who had reappeared while he was on the phone, stared at him as he hung up, shaking her head.

"What?" he grumbled.

"Are you ever going to find a woman?" she asked.

"Are you?" Nate snapped.

She narrowed her eyes. "We're not talking about me. We're talking about you. When are you going to stop making your way through the girls in this town and find yourself a woman?"

He chuckled. "I find plenty of women."

"Yeah, a new one every week. Don't you want someone to love?"

Nate scowled. "Have you been talking to my sister? Because this sounds a lot like a conversation she and I had recently."

Brooke sighed. "No, I haven't been talking to Natasha. We both care about you, though, so we want to see you happy."

"Who says I'm not happy?" he protested. "I'm having fun."

"There's more to life than parties and girls."

He rolled his eyes. "You know what? If I want to talk about my love life, I'll be sure to seek you out. Okay?"

His assistant manager laughed. "You're a piece of work, you know that, right?"

Nate winked. "It's why all the women love me."

"Not all of us, sweetheart," Brooke shot back. She took a deep breath. "I need a break. I'm going to run down to The Percolator for coffee. You want anything?"

"We have coffee here."

"No, we have thick, black goo made by you. I want real coffee made by a trained barista."

Nate made a face. "I'm good."

Brooke dropped her apron on the bar and grabbed her coat off the barstool. "I'll be back in ten. Stay out of trouble."

He threw a towel in Brooke's direction, but she was too far away to hit. Her laughter followed her out the door.

"Am I ever going to find a woman?" he muttered under his breath. "What a stupid question." He turned on the stereo in the corner and punched the volume button until the speakers shook and the window rattled. The music drowned out the constant barrage of annoying questions his brain threw at him. Maybe it would drown out Brooke when she came back.

It had been a long, weird day. After Brooke harassed him about finding love, he moped around, wondering if he was destined to be alone forever. He'd dated tons of women, but none of them made him want anything serious. His relationships—if they could be called that—got shorter with every girl who came along.

He parked on the street in front of his neighbor's house. The driveway was only big enough for two cars. After his sister moved in, they established the "last one home parks on the street" rule. To his permanent irritation, he was almost always the last one home. Late nights were one of the many hazards of owning and running a bar.

Nate was at the front door before he realized he had left his cell phone in his truck. He turned around and jogged back, taking a shortcut across his neighbor's lawn.

It was dark and because he stared at the ground as he headed across the lawn, still contemplating the shit show his love life had become, he didn't see his neighbor until it was too late. He slammed into her, hard enough to make her stumble back a few steps. The bag she had in her arms flew into the air, hit the ground, and burst open, books flying everywhere.

"Oh, shit! I'm sorry," Nate apologized. He dropped to one knee and scooped up several books. His fingers brushed against hers as they reached for the same book, an electric shock jolting him at her touch.

His neighbor yanked her hand back, wincing as if a snake had bitten her. He stared at her, seeing her for the first time.

She was tall, almost as tall as him, with legs that went on for miles. Her blonde hair hung to her waist, her clothes were too large as if she was hiding in them, her glasses were on the end of her nose, and she had a scowl on her face. How the hell had he never noticed her? He couldn't take his eyes off her as she stomped around the yard, grabbing books.

Nate got to his feet and grabbed some books near his feet. He walked across the lawn, stepped in front of her, and held them out to her with a hesitant smile.

She mumbled, "Thank you," took the books, and stacked them with the others.

"Are you okay?" he asked.

"I'm fine." She nodded, her voice barely above a whisper. She didn't look at him as she spoke, then she abruptly spun on her heel and rushed up the lawn to her front door.

"At least let me help you," he called after her.

"No, really, I'm fine," she yelled over her shoulder, even though she jostled the books in her arms as she struggled to unlock her door. "You... you have a good night." She stepped inside and slammed the door closed behind her.

"Perfect," Nate mumbled. "Now women are literally running away from me." He ran a hand through his hair and continued to his car. "Just perfect."

He got his phone and jogged back across his neighbor's yard, glancing at her window as he passed it, wondering if he'd catch another glimpse of her before he went inside. The curtains covering the window made that impossible.

"Hey," Mason called over his shoulder as soon as Nate stepped inside. He was on the couch with an open box of pizza in front of him, a beer, and the baseball game on TV. Exactly what he wanted.

Nate tossed his keys on the table by the door. "Where's Tash?"

"She went out with Avery," Mason answered.

He grinned. "So, I'm off the hook for dinner?"

"Yeah. I know you're upset since you were so excited to go out with us." He shook his head and chuckled. "Grab me another beer, will ya?"

Nate washed his hands and dried them on the towel hanging off the stove, then he opened the fridge, grabbed two beers, and returned to the living room. He handed a beer to Mason, took a slice of pizza, and sat down.

Mason glanced at him. "I need to talk to you," he said.

Nate shot his friend a dirty look. "I swear to God if you mention my love life, I will lay you out flat." He took a huge bite of pizza and chewed aggressively while staring at Mason.

"I'm not going to discuss your love life. Not to mention, your love life is the *last* thing I want to talk about." He put his beer on the table, grabbed the remote, and hit mute. "Me and Tasha are moving out."

The pizza in Nate's mouth was suddenly nothing but a lump of cold dough and congealed cheese. He forced himself to swallow it and took a drink of his beer to wash it down.

"You're... you're moving out?" Nate asked. "Both of you? Together?"

"Yes, both of us." Mason snorted. "We found a place on the other side of town, on the lake. A townhome. You know Van Brooks, right?"

Nate nodded.

"It's his wife's place. She lived there before they got married. Her father owns it and wants to rent it out," Mason explained. "I signed the lease agreement this afternoon."

"Oh. Um, wow." Nate sat back against the couch. "Okay."

"I know it's out of the blue," Mason said. "But Tasha and I have been talking about moving out for a couple of months. You know as well as I do this place is too small for the three of us. We're packed in here like sardines, tripping over each other, bumping into each other." Mason raised an eyebrow. "Overhearing things we don't want to overhear."

Nate exhaled and nodded. "Yeah, I get it. I do. It's weird, though? It never occurred to me you'd move out. I guess I never thought about it."

"We can't be roommates forever," Mason said. "We're not college students anymore, so it's not like we need to live together to save money. The bar is doing great, and the photography studio is picking up steam. We're adults; it's time we moved on to bigger and better things."

"Shit, that sounds scary." Nate chuckled. "But you're right. It probably is long past due for you and Tash to get your own place." He held out his hand. "I'm happy for you guys, bro. Seriously."

Mason shook Nate's hand and smiled. "Thanks." He narrowed his eyes and leaned close to his friend. "You're sure you're okay with this?"

He nodded. "Yeah, I am. My sister loves you. You two are great together. And I can finally have the bachelor's life I was meant to live. It couldn't be more perfect."

Mason grinned and slapped Nate on the back. "I told Tasha you'd be happy for us." He picked up his beer and unmuted the television.

"Yeah," he muttered. "Happy."

Chapter 4
Faith

*F*aith couldn't see where she was going, not only because it was dark, but because the bag of books she struggled to carry blocked her view and her glasses had slid down to the end of her nose, as usual. She prayed she wouldn't stumble like she'd done on multiple occasions, even when she had nothing obstructing her line of sight.

She headed across the lawn, holding the bag in one arm while she attempted to find her keys in the bottom of her backpack. Just as her fingers closed around them, somebody slammed into her, hard enough to make her stumble back a few steps, the bag in her hand tumbling to the ground and bursting open, books flying everywhere.

"Oh, shit, I'm sorry!"

It was Faith's neighbor, the cute one with the short, brown hair, blue eyes, perfect, sexy stubble, and confident gait. Faith figured his good looks were the reason he had a new girlfriend every week. He dropped to one knee at the same time she did and picked up several of the books. His fingers brushed hers as they both reached for the same book, an electric shock jolting her. She yanked her hand away, jumped to her feet, and snatched up the scattered books. When she turned around, her neighbor stood in front of her with books in his hand.

"Thank you," Faith whispered. She refused to make eye contact with him as she gingerly took the books from him and stacked them with the others. She scooped them up and got to her feet.

"Are you okay?" he asked.

She nodded. "I'm fine."

Hoping not to embarrass herself any further, she quickly picked up another book off the sidewalk, spun on her heel, and hurried to her front door, jostling the books in her arms as she battled with the lock.

"At least let me help you," he yelled after her.

"No, really, I'm fine. You... you have a good night." She shoved open the door, stepped inside, and slammed it closed behind her.

Faith tossed the books into the basket by the door, which was already overflowing, and turned on the lights. She pressed her hands to her flushed cheeks. That was the first time she'd spoken to her cute neighbor. He had smiled at her several times, though it was likely more out of politeness than anything else, and she was pretty sure he was the one who had called to her this morning.

Sometimes, she imagined responding to his smiles, flirting with him a little. But that was a dream. If she couldn't make eye contact with him, how could she flirt with him?

Faith shoved herself away from the door with an irritated sigh, pulled off her oversized sweater, and tossed it on the table. She grabbed two of the books off the pile she'd dropped in the basket and examined the spines as she made her way to the kitchen. She'd make some tea and lose herself in one of the new-to-her books for a few hours. It would take her mind off her run-in with her neighbor. He'd probably already forgotten about it.

—

Faith shivered, tucked her blanket around her legs, and snatched her cup off the table, hoping the hot tea would help her warm up. Unfortunately, it was empty.

Fall in Montana brought cooler weather. The weather changed quickly here, and winter swooped in every year, taking her by surprise. Lakeside, Montana, had been her home for six years, and she still hadn't adjusted to the sudden changes in temperatures. Faith couldn't believe there were people here who wore shorts and T-shirts when it was sixty degrees outside. She put on two pairs of socks in the middle of summer.

She picked up Heathcliff and put him on the floor, then she kicked off the blanket and grabbed her empty cup. A loud knock on her front door startled her. Her book fell to the floor, and the cup dropped from her hand onto the coffee table, landing on its side next to her battered copy of *Pride and Prejudice* and the newest Stephen King novel. Nobody ever knocked on her door, except salespeople or someone delivering food, especially at eight in the morning.

Faith jumped off the couch, but her feet tangled in the blanket on the floor and caused her to stumble forward, so she smacked her knee on the corner of the glass coffee table. Heathcliff darted out of her way and escaped into the bedroom.

"Ow," she mumbled under her breath as she limped across the living room to her front door. She balanced on one foot and rubbed her sore knee while she looked through the peephole.

Her neighbor, the cute one she'd collided with the night before, stood on her front stoop, with a cocky smirk on his perfectly chiseled face and his blue eyes flashing with what looked suspiciously like glee. He acted like he belonged there, casually leaning against the rail, a book in his hand.

Faith ducked, forgetting for a second that he couldn't see her. Her breath caught in her throat, and she felt like she was choking as her heart tried to pound its way out of her chest.

This can't be happening.

What the hell was she supposed to say to him? She wasn't sure she could talk to him. Scratch that. She *couldn't* talk to him. She didn't know how to have a conversation with a man. Shoot, she could barely talk to people outside the library.

She glanced in the mirror hanging on the wall to her left and wasn't happy with what she saw—disheveled, dirty blonde hair pulled up in a messy bun, too big glasses that slid down her nose, no makeup, baggy, comfortable clothes, and the look of perpetual confusion she always had on her face.

For a second, she considered not answering the door, but another knock—louder than the first—made her realize she had to open it. She suspected her neighbor would stand there knocking until she opened it and talked to him. Faith took a deep breath, unlocked the door, and opened it far enough to stick her head out.

Her neighbor grinned. "Hi."

The word coupled with his dazzling smile, casual confidence, and gorgeous face almost knocked her off her feet. "H-hello," she squeaked out. Faith cringed as the words left her, and heat rose in her cheeks. Why did she have to sound like a scared mouse? If she was lucky, the floor would open up and swallow her.

"Hi," he repeated.

"C-can I help you?" she asked. Damn it, still squeaking like a mouse.

"I think you dropped this," he said. He held up a book.

"What?"

Good lord, why am I such an idiot?

He laughed and shook his head. "Remember last night, when I crashed into you and your books went flying? I think this is yours. My roommate found it on the sidewalk this morning in front of your house."

Faith reached out and took the book with two fingers, careful not to touch him, remembering the weird shock that rocketed up her arm when they'd touched last night. "Thank you."

She gripped the book in one hand and tried to close the door with the other, but her neighbor stuck his hand through the gap and blurted, "My name is Nate."

Faith eyed him warily, but she reached out and grasped his hand. There were callouses on the pads of some of his fingers, but his grip was bold and confident. It was probably her imagination, but she thought he held onto her a few seconds longer than necessary.

"I'm Faith," she whispered.

Nate's grin widened as he leaned against the doorjamb. One hip jutted out, his brilliant blue eyes sparkling. "It's nice to meet you. I wanted to apologize for last night. I wasn't watching where I was going."

She stepped back. Being close to Nate overwhelmed her, like standing next to the sun. She grabbed the doorknob and squeezed it until her hand hurt.

"It's okay. I... I'm okay. No harm done." She held the book up and wiggled it. "Thanks again. It was, uh, nice to meet you." She slammed the door before Nate said anything else.

Faith thought he would knock again, and if he did, she didn't know what to say to him. She held her breath and leaned against the door. She didn't move or breathe until she felt like her lungs might burst, then she dragged in a deep, cleansing breath and peered through the peephole.

Nate was gone.

Thank God.

Chapter 5

Nate

Nate spent the night thinking about his run-in with his neighbor. He wasn't sure if it was his imagination or what, but there had been some crazy jolt to his system when they'd touched. It stayed with him. He'd woken up with her on his mind.

As soon as he showered and dressed, he headed for the kitchen. Sitting at the center of the table was a book. Nate picked it up and flipped it over to read the back.

"Hey, Mace, where did the book come from?" he yelled. "The one on the table. It doesn't look like your normal World War II read."

Mason stuck his head out of his bedroom door. "I found it on the sidewalk by the street when I went for my run. I don't know how it got there."

"I do," Nate replied. "I'll be right back."

He ran out the front door with the book clutched in his hand before Mason said anything else. He jogged down the driveway and across the lawn, sliding to a stop in front of his neighbor's door. He pushed a hand through his hair and knocked a quick double tap. Then he stepped back, crossed his arms over his chest, and waited.

To his surprise, the conversation with Faith didn't go as he expected. Maybe it was because he'd grown accustomed to sweeping women off their feet, easily charming them with a smile and a wink, but that hadn't happened this time. In fact, she seemed more interested in getting rid of him than chatting with him. The death blow had come when she slammed the door in his face, something that had never happened to him.

That must be why she stayed on his mind. He thought about her on his way to work, while he prepared the bar to open, and even now as he worked, surrounded by attractive women.

How was it he hadn't noticed Faith before? He had no clue how long she'd lived next door, didn't know her name, or anything else about her. He'd seen her coming and going from her house, not that he'd paid much attention. He might have smiled at her once or twice, but he was a friendly person. Things like that happened without him thinking about it.

Natasha came through the front door of the Time Out Bar & Grill and waved at her brother as she made her way through the crowd. She sat on the bar stool across from him, propped her head on her hand, and smiled.

"Hey, big brother," she said. She loved to remind him he was a few minutes older than her.

Nate returned the smile and filled a glass with Sprite. He set it in front of her. "What are you doing here?" he asked.

"Can't I come say hi to my brother?"

He shook his head. "No, because you're the queen of ulterior motives. So, what's up?"

Natasha traced the rim of her glass with her finger. "Mason said he told you we're moving out."

Nate nodded. "He did."

"You're okay with it?" she asked.

"Why wouldn't I be?"

Natasha shrugged. "I thought living alone might, I don't know, bother you."

"Are you kidding?" he said. "I get to walk around in my underwear again, watch what I want on TV, and eat what I want. Plus, I won't have to watch my sister and my best friend making out. Which, by the way, grosses me out."

Natasha laughed and her cheeks turned a light shade of pink. "Sorry about that. I'll tell you what. We'll keep it under control until we move out, okay?"

"Thank God," Nate muttered.

"So, I... uh, heard you broke up with that girl. Mary?" Natasha said.

"You and Brooke have been talking about me, haven't you?" He sighed.

"Yes, but only because we worry about you." She sipped her Sprite. "Are you okay?"

"Yes. Why wouldn't I be?"

She shrugged. "I don't know. I guess... well, it worries me that it doesn't bother you when you break up with someone. It's like it's no big deal."

"It isn't a big deal," he replied. "I only dated her for a couple of weeks."

"You never date anybody for more than a few weeks. Why are you opposed to settling down or dating one woman?" she asked. "What happened that made you afraid to let someone into your life?"

For a split second, Nate considered telling his sister about Elle, spilling his guts and telling her everything he'd held back for the last six years. It might be a relief to tell her about the woman who ripped out his heart and stomped it into oblivion.

"I guess—" He stopped when Natasha leaned forward with an expectant look on her face. He took a breath before he spoke. "I guess I'm not ready to settle down."

"I worry about you," his sister muttered. "Especially with us moving out and leaving you alone."

"Well, don't," he said. "I'm fine. You and Brooke need to stop fussing over me like you're my mother or something."

"Yeah, well, I'm your sister. I think I get to worry."

"There's nothing to worry about. My life is amazing—I've got my bar, I've got my friends, and I've got you. Quit worrying that I'm wasting my life and I'll never be happy. I'm only twenty-seven—"

"We're almost twenty-eight," Natasha interjected.

Nate threw his head back and laughed. "Okay, twenty-eight. Let me live my life. I'll figure it out when I need to figure it out. For now, I'm enjoying myself. Besides, I think I'm done with the serial dating for a while. The stuff you and Mason said about me dating all the women in Lakeside, it kind of hit home. So, I'm taking a break. At least until the right woman falls in my lap."

Or I run into her and almost knock her down.

Natasha clapped her hands and grinned. "Yay! I'm glad to hear that."

"Tell me how you really feel," he grumbled.

Brooke appeared at his side. "What are you glad to hear?" she asked Natasha.

"My brother is going to take a break from dating until he finds the right woman," his sister explained.

Brooke threw her head back and laughed. Her entire body shook, and she couldn't catch her breath. "Oh God, are you serious?"

"Yes, I'm serious." Nate rolled his eyes and crossed his arms over his chest.

Brooke stopped laughing and stepped into Nate's personal space. "Wait a second. What's wrong with you? Are you sick?" She pressed the back of her hand to his forehead, which made Natasha cackle with delight.

He batted Brooke's hand away. "I'm not sick. What's wrong with not dating?"

"For normal people, nothing. For you, sweetie, it's weird."

He rolled his eyes. "You know what? I'm going to excuse myself from this conversation because you're both annoying me. I'm gonna go do some paperwork before I head out for the night. You still good to close?"

"I got it, boss." Brooke winked at him and crossed her arms over her chest.

Nate clapped her on the shoulder and headed upstairs to his office. Halfway up, he glanced back at the bar. Brooke and Natasha had their heads together, talking. Natasha caught him looking and waved at him. He gave her a tight smile before continuing upstairs.

———

For the first time in months, Nate went home alone on a Saturday night. It was a refreshing change to drive home in silence instead of making small talk with a woman he barely knew. Not that he couldn't have found someone; there were plenty of women at the bar more than willing to do anything for the chance to be with him. He wasn't interested. Taking home a different woman week after week had gotten tiresome. He needed a change.

As he turned the corner onto his street, he saw his neighbor crossing her lawn. He pulled to a stop in front of her house and jumped out of the car.

"Faith!" he yelled.

She froze and turned slowly to stare at him as he hurried to her side.

"Hi, there," he said when he caught up with her.

Faith stared at the ground, clutched the book in her hand, and muttered, "Hello."

Nate took a deep breath and inched closer. If only she'd look him in the eye. She wouldn't make it easy on him, though. He touched her arm, and she recoiled, stepping back as if he'd shocked her. He jerked his hand back and stuck it in his pocket.

"Would you like to get a cup of coffee with me sometime?" he asked.

Faith looked confused. She opened her mouth, then closed it again.

"Please, say yes," Nate insisted. "I was thinking we could get to know each other better. I mean, we've lived next door to each other for quite a while, and I only recently learned your name."

"I don't know," she mumbled.

"I promise, no pressure, just coffee." He smiled, hoping he didn't look too eager, or he'd scare her away.

Faith's eyes narrowed, and she sighed. "O-okay, I guess. Coffee sometime. Sure."

Before he could say another word or ask her when she wanted to go, she muttered, "Goodbye," turned on her heel, ran to her door, unlocked it, and darted inside. Nate heard the lock click into place.

At least he got her to agree to the date. He whistled as he made his way across her lawn and up his driveway. He couldn't quite wrap his brain around what he'd done. Three hours ago, he told his sister he didn't want to date anymore. Then he asked his neighbor out.

Inside, he tossed his keys on the table and stepped into the kitchen. Mason and Natasha stood at the counter, scooping food onto plates. Mason glanced at him.

"Why are you grinning?" he asked.

"What?" Nate mumbled.

"You're grinning." Mason chuckled. "I know that look. Did you find some poor, defenseless woman unable to resist your charms as you walked to the front door?"

He grinned and shrugged. "I... uh, I asked our neighbor out for coffee."

Mason narrowed his eyes. "Which neighbor? The woman two houses down? Dude, she's married."

Nate shook his head. "No way! Jesus, Mace, like I'd hit on a married woman." He punched his friend on the shoulder and then pointed helpfully toward Faith's house. "The one who lives right next door."

"Wait, the girl who wears glasses, always has her nose buried in a book, and scurries away like a scared mouse any time anyone talks to her?" Natasha asked. "That neighbor?"

"Yes, that neighbor," Nate replied. "Her name is Faith. That book you found? It was hers. I ran into her a couple of days ago, I mean literally ran into her, which sent her books flying. I returned the book Mace found and introduced myself. Just now, when I pulled up, she was outside, and on impulse, I asked her out."

Mason laughed. "She is *so* not your type."

"Oh, really?" Nate snapped.

"Don't get defensive," Natasha interjected. "Mason is right. She isn't really your type."

"And what exactly *is* my type?"

"Nate—"

He put his hand up, cutting off Mason's protest. "I can't believe this is a serious question. Why do I have to have a type? What's so wrong with me being interested in a woman who goes against my social norm? It might be nice to go out with someone who wasn't half-drunk the moment I met her. I'm tired of meeting women at the bar. Or how about this? I think she's sweet, and I'd like to get coffee with her sometime."

Nate pushed past his sister and best friend and stalked across the living room to his bedroom. He slammed his door; the sound ricocheting through the house. He ignored Mason and Natasha's shouted apologies by turning on the TV in his room and turning up the volume.

The thing was, he wasn't angry with them, not really. They were only voicing the questions lurking in the back of his brain as soon as he asked Faith out. She wasn't his type, not anywhere close, but he'd asked her out. He wasn't sure why, but the second he saw her outside, the idea popped into his head, and once it was there, he couldn't shake it loose.

For the first time in a long time, Nate had experienced the twist of nerves in the pit of his stomach as he waited for Faith's answer. It was an eternity before she'd reluctantly agreed. He suspected she'd said yes to get him to go away.

She had been on his mind since he'd returned her book to her. There was something about her—her reserved smile, the way she clutched her book like it was a lifeline, even how her voice was so low and soft, forcing him to concentrate if he wanted to hear her. Those things fascinated him, and he needed to find out more about her. Tomorrow, he'd talk to her and schedule their coffee date.

Chapter 6

Faith

Faith dropped her backpack and slid to the floor. She wrapped her arms around her legs and rested her head on her knees.

"What the hell just happened?" she muttered to herself.

Somehow, she'd agreed to a coffee date with her adorably cute neighbor. Nate. His name was Nate. It wasn't her fault, really. She hadn't been able to think straight with those intense blue eyes of his boring into her, staring into her soul. She only wanted him to stop looking at her as if he was memorizing her, so she said yes, her mouth getting ahead of her common sense. Now that she was alone, she regretted it.

When had her life turned into a cheesy romantic comedy? Guys who looked like Nate, guys who could have any girl they wanted, didn't go out with girls like her. They didn't act interested in her or ask her out for coffee.

Maybe it was a joke, or he lost a bet with one of his friends or somebody at his bar. That was probably the reason he asked her out.

Faith got to her feet and looked out the window next to the door. Her front yard was empty. She threw the deadbolt and slipped the chain into place before she went to the kitchen, where she took a cup from the cupboard to make tea. She leaned against the counter, with Heathcliff weaving between her legs while she waited for the electric kettle to warm the water.

"I can't go out with Nate," she said out loud. Heathcliff looked up at her and meowed before he disappeared down the hall.

The thought of a date with her neighbor terrified her. How the hell was she going to get out of it?

Faith was painfully shy, had been since she was a child. It was why her nose was always buried in a book. It was her way of hiding in plain sight. If she went out with Nate, she wouldn't know what to say, how to act, and she wouldn't be able to function like a normal person. Not to mention the stares of the other coffee shop patrons, judging her, wondering how and why he was with her. It would be nothing short of embarrassing for both of them.

A million reasons not to go out with him ran through her head. But the one that stood out more than any other was her inexperience with men. She hadn't dated since high school, and that had been a brief, disastrous relationship during her senior year. It left such a nasty taste in her mouth that she hadn't dated since, making it nine years since she had been on a date. Faith kept her heart locked down, refusing to let anyone in, aside from a few close friends. It was easier to protect herself when she didn't open herself up to heartache.

It would be for the best if she stayed home with her cat and her books. They never let her down.

There had to be a way out of it. While she couldn't deny there was a physical attraction, she wasn't prepared to date Nate. Forget that she could get lost in those blue eyes of his or drown in the perfect pitch of his voice. The attraction was purely physical, nothing more. She'd come up with some excuse to not have coffee with him—dead grandparent, sick cat, or maybe she'd claim she was sick.

She couldn't go out with Nate, even if it had the potential to be a perfect date. Tomorrow, she'd tell him the date was off.

—

For the third morning in a row, Faith was late. To make matters worse, she discovered she was out of coffee, which meant a stop at The Percolator. It was becoming a habit she couldn't break. On her way out the door, she grabbed her latest read off the kitchen table and shoved it in her over-sized purse. Halfway down the sidewalk, she looked down and realized her slippers were on her feet. With a sigh, she turned around and went back inside.

Five minutes later, she had on shoes instead of slippers and was on her way to the coffee shop. Unfortunately, half-asleep college students desperate to wake up filled The Percolator, so the line stretched from the counter to the door. Faith got in it, opened her purse, and pulled out her book. It would be a while before she got her coffee.

As she inched forward, she heard the door open, and someone got in line behind her.

"Hi there," a deep voice said in her left ear.

Faith jumped, squeaked like a mouse, and dropped her book. She bent down to get it, but a hand reached past her and snagged it first. She stood upright and came face to face with Nate.

He wiggled his fingers in a cute little wave and put her book into her hands. "Good morning."

She clutched it tight and stared at him.

He chuckled and pointed at his chest. "Nate," he said. "Your neighbor."

"I know who you are," she blurted. She immediately regretted it; she hadn't meant to sound so harsh. She closed her eyes and exhaled. "Sorry. Um, hi."

She spun around and held her breath, hoping he wouldn't try to talk to her or expect her to have a conversation with him.

The line moved, and she moved with it. She put her book in front of her face, but she couldn't concentrate on it. Once she got to the counter, she ordered her coffee, but before she could pay, Nate reached around her and dropped a twenty-dollar bill in front of the barista.

"I got it," he said. "Mine and hers. Large Americano, hot, no cream or sugar. Keep the change."

"You didn't have to do that," Faith whispered.

Nate's smile dazzled her. "Just so you know, this doesn't count as our coffee date." He took his drink from the barista, nodded at Faith, and left.

"Do you know that guy?" the barista asked as she handed Faith her drink.

She shrugged. "He's... he's my neighbor," she mumbled.

"He's cute," the barista said.

She nodded, then she turned around and bolted out the door.

Outside, she looked up and down the street, but Nate was gone. She got into her car, started the engine, and drove to work, chastising herself for the entire drive.

Was Nate flirting with me?

Faith couldn't tell when someone flirted with her. In fact, she was oblivious to it. Not that it happened often, if ever.

She pulled into her parking spot behind the library, grabbed her things, and headed inside. She tripped on the edge of the concrete stairs leading up to the door and almost dropped her coffee. Some of it sloshed over the side of the cup when she hit her elbow on the door as it swung closed. She cursed under her breath.

"Good morning, Faith," Caroline called from the front counter.

"Hello," she yelled back. Once she stashed her things in her desk drawer, she headed out front.

Caroline stood on a stepstool in the non-fiction section a few feet from the main checkout counter. She balanced a stack of books on one arm and returned them to the shelf with the other. She hummed a nameless tune under her breath as she worked.

"Do you need some help?" Faith asked.

Caroline jumped, the books in her hand tottering precariously. She put them down and shook her head. "Yeah, don't scare the crap out of me."

Faith giggled. "Sorry."

"It's okay. Anyway, I'm good down here."

"Well, if you need me, I'll be upstairs, shelving books." She turned to go.

"Will you check the workrooms while you're up there?" Caroline asked. "Several study groups were here late last night and there are books everywhere."

Faith nodded and headed to the second floor. Workrooms suitable for small study groups lined one side of the library's second floor. Shelves of reference books filled the other side of the expansive room. Sure enough, two of the rooms had books stacked haphazardly on the tables, as well as some on the floor.

Faith grabbed a rolling cart from behind the desk and pushed it into the first room. Her mind drifted as she stacked the books on the cart.

Nate surprised her when he bought her coffee this morning. While she'd planned to cancel their date, she never got around to it. Instead, she'd done her best to avoid running into him. She looked outside for his car before she left, didn't get out of her car until she made sure no one else was around, and even then, she ran to and from her front door. She had been avoiding him, hoping if she didn't see him or talk to him, the date wouldn't happen.

Maybe he was being nice.

Except, men—people—weren't nice to her. Faith could count the number of people who treated her with kindness over the years on one hand. None of them were of the male persuasion. She had a deep-rooted suspicion of anyone who did anything for her, stemming from her shitty childhood and a mother who was better at manipulating her child than raising her.

Faith closed her eyes and took several deep breaths, a trick her therapist told her to use when her anxiety got the best of her. Any time she thought about her mom, her anxiety skyrocketed. Today was no exception.

She set the pile of books in her arms on the table and sat down. It had been a while since she thought about her mother. The woman hadn't been a part of her life for almost ten years. When Faith was twelve, she'd been put in foster care. For the next four years, she had bounced from group home to group home, with occasional visits from her mother, and even one attempt to move back home that lasted less than a week. At sixteen, she emancipated herself, and the day after graduating high school, she packed her measly belongings into a thrift store suitcase and bought a bus ticket to wherever the money in her pocket would take her. It turned out to be Missoula, Montana.

Faith lived in Missoula for six months until chance brought her into the path of Margaret Hudspeth—Maggie, for short. Maggie was a professor at Lakeside College. She had been spending the summer in Missoula teaching at the University of Montana. Maggie frequented the coffee shop where Faith worked, and they struck up a friendship. When she told the professor about her dream of becoming a librarian, Maggie offered to help her in any way possible. The next thing she knew, Faith was in Lakeside, working as an assistant librarian-in-training and going to school for free. She owed her new life to Maggie, and she was beyond grateful for everything her new friend helped her achieve.

After she graduated from Lakeside College with a master's degree in Library and Information Sciences, Faith stayed in Lakeside. She loved the little town and the Flathead Lake area. After six years, it was her home.

Faith got to her feet. Enough reminiscing, she had work to do. After work, she had big plans to hide in her house and read her book.

Chapter 7

Faith

Mission accomplished.

Faith avoided Nate all weekend. It wasn't difficult; she stayed inside and didn't leave, not even when Caroline called and suggested they go to Kalispell for dinner and a movie. By Sunday night, she had no doubt he'd completely forgotten about the coffee date.

Monday started off on the right foot. For once, she made it out of the house on the first try—keys, shoes, clothes, and purse where they were supposed to be. Nate's car was in front of her house, a normal occurrence after the girl Faith suspected was his sister moved in with them. Thankfully, he wasn't anywhere to be seen. She hurried down the sidewalk, quickly got in her car, and started it, but when she tried to put it in drive, the gearshift wouldn't move. She tried again, but still nothing. She shut off the car.

"Shit." Faith rested her forehead on the steering wheel and tried not to cry. This wasn't happening. She'd spent what little money she had saved on new tires three months ago. If something was wrong with the damn thing, she couldn't afford to fix it.

A tap on the window made her jump. When she turned her head to see who it was, Nate wiggled his fingers in a tiny wave. She sighed and opened the door.

"Car trouble?"

Faith bit her lip and nodded. She swallowed and said, "Yeah. I don't know what's wrong with it, but I'm going to be late for work."

He tipped his head toward his truck. "Come on, I'll give you a ride."

She thought about saying no, but she needed to get to the library. Caroline was on her way to Missoula for the day, leaving Faith in charge. She *had* to get to work. Worrying about her car would have to wait. She grabbed her things and followed him to his truck. He unlocked it with the remote on his keys and opened the passenger door for her. She glanced at him out of the corner of her eye and pulled herself into the truck. Nate shut the door, jogged around the front of the vehicle, and got in.

"I, uh, I'm sorry," he said. "I don't know where you work."

Faith clutched her hands in her lap and stared at them. "The library," she whispered.

He shook his head and chuckled under his breath.

"What?" she asked.

"Nothing," he replied.

She rolled her eyes. She knew she gave off stereotypical vibes—the books, the glasses, the bun in the hair—it screamed "librarian." It hadn't occurred to her how strong those vibes were until Nate laughed at her. Heat rushed to her cheeks, and she squeezed her hands together so tight her knuckles turned white. Faith felt the weight of his gaze on her, but she stared straight ahead, chewing on the inside of her cheek.

He cleared his throat. "I shouldn't have laughed. I'm sorry."

"You're full of apologies, aren't you?" she muttered.

He shook his head and hit the button on the door to roll down the window a few inches, letting the cold air into the truck's cab. "Yes, I am. I'm sorry I don't know where you work and that I laughed."

Faith sighed. "First, there's no reason for you to know where I work. We're neighbors who know nothing about each other. Second, I know I scream 'librarian' when you look at me."

"Actually, I figured you were a librarian because you obviously love books," Nate explained. "You always have one in your hand, you have stacks of them in your house, and when I ran into you, I knocked a bunch of books out of your arms. It seemed logical. It has nothing to do with how you look."

She peeked at him out of the corner of her eye. He was so relaxed. He drove with his wrist propped on the steering wheel, the wind from the open window tousling his hair, and he had a pleasant smile on his face. She couldn't see his eyes behind his dark sunglasses, which made it hard to figure out what he was thinking.

"Coffee?"

"Wh-what?"

"Let's get some coffee," he said.

Without waiting for her to answer, he made an abrupt right-hand turn and drove down Adams Street. He parked in front of The Percolator, shut off the engine, and jumped out. Faith reached for the door, but Nate was already there, pulling it open and holding out his hand. She took it and let him help her out of the truck. He slammed the door before she could grab her purse.

"My purse—"

"I got it," he said. "Don't worry about it."

Inside, they got in line behind the usual college students and people commuting to Kalispell. Faith hung back, standing behind him until he turned around, took her by the elbow, and guided her to stand next to him.

At the counter, Nate smiled at the barista and ordered himself a large Americano and a large hot vanilla latte.

"How did you know to order that?" Faith asked after he paid.

Nate smirked. "I overheard you the other day. You seem like someone who has a routine and stays consistent."

"You remembered what I ordered?"

He shrugged and, to her surprise, his cheeks turned pink. They stepped to the side to wait for their drinks.

"I don't always order the same thing," she murmured.

He looked at her, one eyebrow raised. "So, I got it wrong?"

Faith shook her head. "No. But sometimes I order tea, or something with caramel; once I even tried their pumpkin spice latte." She shrugged. "I thought you should know I'm not completely predictable."

Nate didn't have time to respond because the barista set their drinks on the counter. He grabbed both of them and carefully handed her the steaming hot drink. He held the door open and as she passed him, then he put his hand in the middle of her back and guided her to the truck. A tingle ran down her spine.

They were both quiet as Nate drove through town to the library. Faith directed him to the back parking lot when they arrived. He pulled into a spot close to the door and, to Faith's chagrin, parked next to the library's student worker, Paisley, who was still in her car.

She reached for the door handle, but he put his hand on her arm, stopping her. "I know an excellent mechanic. I'll talk to him."

She rubbed her forehead and sighed. "I don't know," she mumbled.

"Why don't I pick you up when you get off and take you home? Kane can stop on his way home and look at your car. Sound good?"

"You don't have to do that."

"Do you know someone who fixes cars?" Nate asked.

Faith froze, realizing she didn't know anyone. She reluctantly shook her head. "No, I... I don't know anybody."

"Well, Kane owes me a favor. Let me help you. Please?"

"Okay," she mumbled. She didn't have a choice; she needed her car. "I'm off work at six."

"I'll be here."

She opened the door, gathered her things, and jumped out. Nate shouted goodbye after her, but she slammed the door and cut him off. She ran to the back door of the library, digging through her purse for her keys.

Paisley met her at the door. She looked over her shoulder at Nate's truck, then she leaned close to Faith and whispered, "Was that the guy who owns the Time Out Bar?"

"Yes," she replied. "He's my neighbor. I had car trouble this morning, so he gave me a ride to work."

Paisley's eyes widened. "Nate is your neighbor? Lucky."

"Yes," she said. She closed her eyes. "Is he still there?"

"Yep." Paisley giggled. "I think he's waiting for us to go inside."

"Dammit." Faith's hand shook as she put the key in the lock. It took three tries to get it unlocked. As soon as the door opened, she darted into the building.

"Are you okay?" Paisley asked.

Faith leaned against the wall. "No. I don't know how to talk to him. He makes me nervous." She pinched the bridge of her nose.

Paisley patted her arm. "He is extremely attractive. He makes my friends nervous, so I understand why he makes you nervous. But he's human, just like anyone else. You should ask him out on a date." She turned and walked away.

Faith leaned against the wall and closed her eyes. How could Paisley be so nonchalant about something like that? There was no way she'd ask Nate out, not in a million years. Thinking about it made her want to vomit, as did the thought of riding home with him and letting him help her with her car.

How was she going to get out of that? The better question was, how the hell had she gotten herself into this situation?

Chapter 8

Nate

"Thanks, Kane. I appreciate it. I'll see you in an hour." Nate ended the call and tucked his phone in his front pocket. He turned around and bumped into Brooke. She grinned at him.

"You're leaving?" she asked. "Did your truck break down?"

"No," he replied, dragging out the word. "Why?"

"Because I heard you ask Kane to meet you at your place," she said. "Why else would you need a mechanic?"

He crossed his arms over his chest and glared at his assistant manager. "You were eavesdropping?"

Brooke grabbed a tray, opened the cooler, and took out several bottles of beer. "Maybe a little. So, did your truck break down or not?"

"You saw it in the parking lot, so you know it didn't." Nate picked up a cloth and wiped down the bar so he didn't have to look at his assistant manager. She had an uncanny knack for getting information out of him. "My neighbor's car isn't working. I'm helping her out."

"By asking Kane to come to your place? That's a bit more than helpful. Why doesn't she take it to his shop?" Brooke put her hands on her hips and smirked. "Or is this you making a move on some poor, unsuspecting female? I thought you were done with dating for a while? Or is your neighbor one of the few women in this town you haven't dated?"

"Stop it," Nate grumbled.

"What?"

"Don't make assumptions," he snapped. "I feel bad for her and I want to help."

Brooke put her hands up and took a step back. "Okay, fair enough. Are you coming back after you help her?"

He could almost hear the quotation marks around the word "help." He rolled his eyes. "Aw, sarcasm. Shocking, especially from you." Nate checked the clock on the wall. "Yeah, I'll try to be back by eight."

Brooke nodded, took the tray loaded with beers, and walked away. He dug his keys out of his pocket and headed for the door.

Ten minutes later, he parked at the back of the library. He kept the truck running and the heat on. Fall in Montana was chilly, and in the last few days, the temperature had dropped. He'd noticed Faith wearing a heavy sweatshirt this morning, so he wanted it to be warm for her.

At 6:03 p.m., the door opened, and she walked out. She stopped, looked around, and when she saw Nate in his truck, her shoulders slumped before she trudged across the lot. He jumped out and jogged around to open the door for her.

"Hi," he said.

"H-hello," she whispered as she climbed in and folded her hands in her lap.

"How was your day?" he asked once he was back in the truck.

"Um, it was good, thanks," she mumbled. "How was yours?"

Nate shrugged. "Not bad. I have to go back to work after Kane looks at your car, so it's not exactly over."

"You mentioned Kane earlier. He's a mechanic?"

"Yeah. He's a friend of mine, and he owns Lakeside Automotive. He agreed to stop by on his way home from work."

Faith shook her head. "Oh, no, he doesn't have to do that. I don't want him to go out of his way for me."

"I told you he owes me a favor. It's okay."

As they came around the corner, he saw Kane's car in front of his house. He parked behind him and got out. They met at the truck and shook hands.

"You're early," Nate said.

"My last customer showed up ten minutes ago. So, I thought I'd head over," Kane replied.

"Great." Nate turned to Faith, who had gotten out of the truck while they talked. "Kane, this is my neighbor, Faith. It's her car."

Kane raised a hand. "Hey, there. What's wrong with it?"

"My check engine light came on," she explained. "And when I put it in gear, it won't move."

"Have you noticed any unusual noises?" he asked. "Does it make a weird grinding or whining noise? Especially when you're speeding up or slowing down?"

Faith nodded. "I've heard both sounds, whining and grinding."

"Can you pop the hood?" Kane asked.

She went to her car, unlocked it, and got in. Nate heard a clunk, and the hood opened a few inches. Kane propped it open and leaned down.

"Nate, you got a flashlight?"

"Yep." He grabbed one from behind the seat in the truck and tossed it to Kane.

Kane looked under the hood, then he lay on his back and slid under the car. After a few minutes, he crawled out and stood up. "I'm not positive, but I think it might be your transmission. I need to take it to my shop to get a good look at it. I'll have one of my guys come tow it down there tomorrow, if you want?"

"How much is that going to cost?" Faith asked.

"I won't know until I get it in the shop," Kane said.

"Um..."

"I'll pay to have it towed," Nate interjected.

Faith shook her head. "You don't have to."

"Will you excuse us?" Nate said to Kane. He took Faith's elbow and guided her up the sidewalk a few feet from her car.

She shifted from foot to foot and twisted her hands in front of her. "You shouldn't have offered to pay," she mumbled.

"I want to help," he insisted.

Faith moved to protest, but Nate held up his hand. "I know you don't want my help. I don't know if you think I'm insincere or that I have some ulterior motive, but honestly, I don't. One neighbor helping the other. I'll cover the towing charge, and that's it. I swear."

She wouldn't make eye contact with him; instead, she stared at the ground. After a few seconds, she muttered, "Okay," so quietly Nate had trouble hearing her.

"Great. I, um, need your car key," he said, holding out his hand. "I'll give you a ride to the library until it's fixed."

Faith sighed as she took her house key off the keyring and handed her car key to him. "I don't work tomorrow," she whispered.

"Okay, no ride tomorrow," he said. "Hold on while I talk to Kane. I'll be right back."

Nate jogged down the sidewalk, gave Kane the key, and made plans for him to pick up the car the next day. They said their goodbyes, and Kane got in his car and left. When Nate turned around, Faith was gone. He saw light through the window by the door. He considered going to the door and knocking, but he decided against it. Obviously, she didn't want to speak to him, or she'd have waited. Maybe she needed a break, so he would give it to her. He returned to his truck to go back to work.

—

Nate stayed until the bar closed and waited for the parking lot to empty before he left. He wasn't in the mood to talk to anybody. He drove home in silence, lost in his thoughts.

At home, he had to weave through a maze of boxes to get to the couch. He turned on *Sportscenter* and stared at the TV without really comprehending what was on the screen.

Mason stuck his head out of his bedroom door and smiled at him. "Hey, how's it going?"

"Great," he muttered. "Why are you up so late? It's almost two."

"I'm reading," Mason replied. He stepped out and pulled the door closed. "Dude, you don't look so good. Are you sick?"

Nate snorted. "No."

Mason sat next to him and stared at him until Nate shifted away from him.

"Knock it off," he snapped.

Mason grinned. "I'm not doing anything."

"You're doing that thing where you stare at me until I crack. Like you did when Melody Olson cheated on me in high school, but I didn't want to talk about it." Nate crossed his arms and glared at his best friend.

"Or when Elle got married," Mason mumbled.

Nate recoiled. They didn't talk about Elle. It was an unwritten rule. She was off-limits.

"Watch it," he sneered.

"I'm sorry," Mason replied. "But you've been kind of mopey. Right now, you look like your dog died."

"Fine, I'll tell you what's bothering me, but you cannot laugh, and you *cannot* tell my sister."

Mason sat back and nodded. "Okay."

"Our neighbor? I don't think she likes me." Nate explained what happened earlier, starting with Faith's car trouble and ending with her disappearing into her house without a word.

"Wow," Mason said when he finished talking.

"See? She doesn't like me."

Mason chuckled and shook his head. "Has it occurred to you she might be shy?"

"What?"

"Shy, Nathaniel. I know you don't come across many of them down at the bar, but they exist. I don't know much about her, but I get the impression she's shy. She never makes eye contact with anybody. She's lived next door for years, and none of us have talked to her, and she keeps to herself. Getting attention from you is probably overwhelming."

Nate raised an eyebrow. "I'm not overwhelming."

"Not to the college girls hanging out at Time Out on the weekends, but to the quiet, shy woman living next door? Yeah, you are." Mason shrugged. "You're used to women falling for any line you feed them. You never have to work to get the girl. This time you might. Give her time, she'll come around."

"I think I like this woman," he murmured. "She's not like anyone I've ever dated before."

Mason grinned. "Then you should wait for her."

Nate scrubbed a hand over his face. "I'll wait. But it's weird. I've never done this before."

Mason clapped him on the back. "Welcome to the real world, buddy. It sucks."

Chapter 9

Faith

The tow truck was at her house at seven a.m. on the dot. Faith heard the telltale beep as it backed up and positioned itself in front of her car. She peeked out the window and saw Nate standing on his lawn, watching as they loaded her car onto the flatbed and drove away.

Nate glanced at her house before he climbed into his truck. She didn't bother to open the door. Instead, she returned to the living room, pulled the blanket from the back of the couch over her legs, and opened her book.

It was impossible to concentrate on the words on the page, not when Nate kept invading her thoughts. She couldn't understand why he was being so nice to her. Maybe it was a cruel joke.

It wasn't like it hadn't happened before. Growing up in the foster care system and bouncing from home to home had taught her the only person she could trust was herself. After her emancipation at sixteen, she'd lived in a local shelter owned by friends of her former case manager. They allowed her to stay in a tiny, closet-sized room in exchange for helping around the shelter—cleaning, laundry, even lawn work. Faith studied hard and kept to herself, intent on leaving Texas as soon as she graduated high school. The only friend she had was the niece of the owner, a girl named Connie, who was a year younger than her.

Three months before the end of the school year and Faith's escape from Texas, Connie found out Faith had a crush on a classmate. What followed was a whirlwind romance orchestrated by Connie, a romance that left Faith crying on her bedroom floor after a public break-up and shaming session used to remove her from his life. Only after being completely humiliated, she learned he'd only asked her out because Connie dared him to, and he kept dating her because he wanted to get her into bed. Her refusal to have sex with him led to her public humiliation.

Ever since, a deep distrust lingered, coloring her perception of any man's attention, making her convinced no one genuinely cared for her. While she desperately wanted Nate to be different, history had taught her it wasn't usually the case.

Faith closed her eyes. She needed to stop thinking about him. It was her day off, and as much as she loved her job at the library, she enjoyed the days she got to hang out at home with nothing to do but read her books and relax with Heathcliff.

Forty-five minutes later and several chapters into her book, there was a knock on her door, followed immediately by Nate calling her name. Faith closed her eyes and wondered if it was possible to ignore him.

"I know you're in there," he yelled. "You might as well open the door. I'm not going anywhere until you do."

She contemplated not getting up, but she was sure Nate intended to follow through with his promise to stand out there until she acknowledged him. With a sigh, she shoved the blanket off, put her book on the table, and walked across the living room to her door.

A grin spread across his face when she opened it. "Hi," he said.

His smile intoxicated her, which drove her crazy. She didn't want to fall under his spell. He was all wrong for her.

"Hi," Faith replied warily. "What are you doing here?"

Nate held up a drink carrier loaded with five precariously balanced drinks. "Can I come in?" he asked.

"Why?"

"It will only be for a few minutes. I promise," he said. "Give me ten minutes and then, if you want me to leave, I will."

Her first instinct was to close the door, but his smile, coupled with his sparkling blue eyes, made him irresistible. Faith stepped back and gestured for him to come in.

As she closed the door behind him, she had to swallow back the urge to vomit. Nate was in her house, walking toward her kitchen. He pushed a stack of books out of his way and put the drink carrier on the table. He appeared calm, confident, and as if being there was the most natural place for him to be. She inched closer, curious about what he was up to.

"Since I haven't been able to convince you to go get coffee with me, I brought the coffee to you," Nate said. "I remembered you like different things, so I got a variety— black tea, that pumpkin spice thing you mentioned, a vanilla latte like you had yesterday, and a caramel macchiato. The black coffee is mine." He removed each drink from the carrier as he described it and lined them up on the table. Then he sat down and smiled at her.

Faith's smile spread across her face as she shook her head. "You're crazy," she murmured.

Nate chuckled. "I know. Anyway, I thought you'd be more comfortable here, away from the crowds of people."

It shocked her that he apparently knew what she wanted all along. It would be easier, a date away from public scrutiny. The least she could do was give him a chance. She eased into the chair across from him, reached over, and picked up the caramel macchiato.

Nate took the black coffee and leaned back, sprawled in his seat like he belonged there. "Does that mean I don't have to leave?"

"You don't have to leave," Faith replied. She grabbed her sweatshirt off the back of the chair and pulled it on, burying herself in its oversized comfort, like a security blanket. Taking a deep, cleansing breath did nothing to stop her shaking hands or pounding heart. She sipped the coffee and peered at Nate over the top of the cup.

His eyes drifted around the house. "You really have a lot of books," he said.

Faith laughed, and a blush heated her cheeks. That was an understatement. Every inch of space was merely another place to put her books. Books overflowed everywhere—her tiny bookshelf, her kitchen table, the coffee table in the living room, and multiple baskets around the house. She meant to get rid of the ones she'd already read, but it never happened.

She pointed at herself. "Librarian, remember? Yes, it's cliché, but I love to read."

"I think it's refreshing," he said.

"Oh?"

Nate rubbed a hand over the back of his neck and shrugged. "The last few girls I dated, well, I'm not sure they ever read a book, unless it was for school. Books and reading weren't their thing."

"Those are my *only* things," she mumbled. "They have been my entire life. It was how I escaped from reality when I was younger and life wasn't... well, so great for me. Books are the one thing that makes me happy."

Nate rested his arms on the table, his complete attention on her. She didn't know how long she could handle those baby blue eyes staring at her or listen to his rich, full voice without fainting or possibly dying. It was hard to believe he was in her kitchen at her table, talking and listening to her as if it were the most natural thing in the world. Like he belonged there.

He looked around with an appraising eye. "You need more bookshelves."

"I know," she agreed. "But I don't have time to get any." Faith took a sip of her coffee and cleared her throat. She might as well make the best of their impromptu date. Not that she was good at this kind of thing, but there was nothing wrong with trying.

"Wh-what about you? What's your *thing*?" she asked.

He laughed, the sound filling the room. Nate made a cute "I'm concentrating" face before he answered.

"You know what? I thought I knew what it was, but lately, I'm not so sure." He looked at the top of his coffee cup and lowered his voice. "I studied business in school, and I own arguably the most popular bar and grill in a hundred-mile radius, but I don't feel … fulfilled. Sometimes, it feels like something is missing or, I don't know, off. I wish I knew what it was, but I don't have a clue."

He seemed so vulnerable that without letting herself think about it, Faith reached over and squeezed his hand, startled when that crazy electric jolt rushed up her arm. Nate must have felt it as well because his smile faltered the tiniest bit, replaced briefly with a look of confusion. It passed quickly, and his smile returned.

"I should go. I need to get to work," he whispered. "I'm sorry I barged in here and forced you to drink coffee with me."

She grinned. "It wasn't so bad. I… I enjoy talking to you."

"That's good to hear." Nate got to his feet.

Faith narrowed her eyes. "Why?"

"Because I plan on taking you out for a proper date," he said as he walked to the front door.

She jumped up and followed him, intent on telling him she didn't need another pity date. Before she could, he stopped and turned to her with that damn smirk on his face.

"And I will give you a ride to work until Kane fixes your car. That was our deal, right?" Nate winked at her, threw open the door, and bounded down the steps. Halfway across the lawn, he looked back and yelled, "See you tomorrow!"

Faith closed the door, then she pressed her hands to her warm cheeks.

Did we just have our first date?

She wasn't sure if that counted as a date, but she knew she couldn't wait to see him again.

Chapter 10

Nate

Nate wasn't looking forward to telling Faith about his conversation with Kane. Her car repairs would cost almost $2000. Not that he was surprised. Every day that passed without a phone call from Kane made him worry that the cost had reached astronomical numbers and was too expensive to fix. By the time Friday rolled around, Nate wondered if it was even fixable. Now he had to deliver the bad news, and based on what he'd gleaned during their drive-to-work conversations this week, Faith couldn't afford a bill that large.

The music from the party at his house followed him as he trudged across Faith's lawn and up her sidewalk. After he tapped on her door, there was an enormous crash, and the cat meowed before Faith opened the door with her glasses propped on her head, sweater hanging to her knees, and mismatched socks. Nate bit his tongue and smiled.

Faith was chaotic in a way he found utterly adorable. The more time he spent with her, the more he liked her.

"Um ... hi," she mumbled. Her brows furrowed, and she gnawed on her lower lip. "What are you doing here? Did I leave something in the truck?"

Nate shook his head. "No."

"Oh, well, I didn't expect to see you until Monday. What's up?"

"Can I come in?" he asked.

Faith nodded, a bit too vigorously, which sent her glasses flying off her head. Nate reached out and snatched them mid-air before they hit the floor. He handed them to her as he stepped inside and shut the door.

"I talked to Kane about your car," Nate said. "He apologized for having it so long, but he had some family issues come up this week." He cleared his throat. "Anyway... he said it's uh... well, it's going to cost two grand to fix."

Faith's mouth dropped open. She snapped it closed, and tears welled in her eyes. Abruptly, she spun around and darted into the kitchen. She grabbed a napkin off the counter and pressed it to her face. Nate stood back and waited.

After a few minutes, Faith straightened up and turned back to him. "I'm sorry about that," she whispered. "I didn't expect that."

"It's a lot."

"It's more than I have," she said. "A lot more." She exhaled shakily. "I don't know what I'm going to do."

Nate took a step closer. "We'll come up with something."

Faith sighed and looked at the floor. "You've already done so much. I can't ask you to do anything else."

He stepped into the kitchen, caught her hand in his, and gently squeezed it. "I want to help. You're my friend. At least, I'd like to *think* you're my friend."

She nodded and her shoulders relaxed. "You're so sweet. What did I do to deserve a friend like you?"

Nate chuckled. "Ran into me with a bag of books."

Faith wiped her face and tossed the napkin in the trash. "I guess that was a good thing, huh?"

"I think it was," he whispered.

Faith pulled her hand from his, went to the sink, filled a glass with water, and quickly downed it. When she turned back to him, she seemed steadier and more balanced.

"I'll figure out how to get the money," she said. "Or I'll buy a bike."

Nate laughed. "You will not be riding a bike in the winter."

Faith shrugged. "Then I guess I'll call my neighbor to give me a ride." As soon as the words were out of her mouth, she blushed and looked down. "That was a joke."

"I know." He rocked back and forth on his toes for a second, knowing he needed to leave. He wanted to stay, but he wouldn't unless Faith asked him to. When she didn't, he clapped his hands together once and turned to leave. "I guess I'll go."

She followed him, standing back as he opened the door and stepped outside. The music from his house hit them immediately. The party was in full swing. He turned back to Faith.

"Would you like to come over? We're having a going-away party for my sister and Mason. They're getting their own place. BBQ, beer, and baseball on the TV. Why don't you join us?"

She shook her head before he finished talking. "I... I don't think so."

"Are you sure? It'll be fun."

"Would it count as our date?" she asked with a grin.

"Absolutely not," Nate scoffed. "Our first date will not be with a bunch of my drunk friends and my *sister*."

Faith giggled. "I'm not getting out of that date, am I?"

"Nope." Nate reached out, grabbed her hand, and gave it a gentle squeeze. "I'll talk to you later." He stopped with his hand on the knob. "Last chance?"

"No, really. I'm good. I'll see you on Monday."

Faith locked the door behind him. He stood on her porch for a few minutes, his head resting against the door, wishing Faith trusted him, wondering for the millionth time in the last week how he *could* gain her trust. After a few minutes, he strode back across the lawn to his house.

The music thumped in the center of his brain, making his eyes throb. He opened the door, the blaring music smacking him in the face, along with the noise of thirty people talking and laughing. Someone had already started a beer can pyramid on the kitchen table, and the baseball game played on the TV, competing with the other noises in the room. His friends shouted his name, and his sister waved at him from her perch on Mason's shoulders.

Nate waved back before he grabbed a plate and loaded it with food. Then he squeezed onto the couch between Oscar and Gavin. He watched the game without paying attention—neither team was his favorite—and thought about Faith. As much as he liked these people, right now, he wanted to be with her.

"Why are you making that face?" Natasha asked as she plopped down on the coffee table in front of him.

He sighed. "What face?"

"Your sad, grumpy face. If anybody should want to party louder than anybody here, it's you," she said. "By the end of the month, you'll have this place to yourself, and you can turn it into the bachelor pad you've always wanted."

Nate raised an eyebrow. "Who said I wanted a bachelor pad?"

"What single guy doesn't want a bachelor pad?" Natasha laughed.

"This one."

"You're funny." Natasha giggled, messed up her brother's hair, then bounded to her feet, and shouted Mason's name.

Gavin gave him an odd look. "You're not pumped about finally having this place to yourself?"

He shrugged. "Not really, no."

"But you'll be able to bring home any girl you want, judgment-free," Oscar added.

Nate sighed. "Yeah, well, I'm kind of sick of the 'dating a different woman every week' thing."

Gavin's eyebrows shot up. "Our resident ladies' man doesn't want the job anymore? Or did you finally date every woman in Lakeside?"

"You guys need new jokes," Nate muttered. "For the record, I haven't dated *every* woman in Lakeside, and yes, I think I'm sick of being a ladies' man. I want to find a nice girl to date, you know, for more than a few weeks."

Gavin slapped him on the back. "Good for you."

"Why does that sound condescending?" Nate asked.

Gavin didn't answer because somebody on the TV hit a home run, distracting him. With his friend's attention on the TV, Nate got up, dumped his half-full plate of food in the trash, and grabbed a beer from the fridge. He returned to the couch where he sat sucking on it, watching the chaos around him.

After the game ended, he snatched another drink and moved to the chair in the corner. When Natasha walked past him, he grabbed her arm.

"Can I ask you something?" he asked.

"Yeah, sure. What's up?"

He explained what he wanted to do. She stared at him for a few minutes, tapping her finger against her chin. "Yeah, I think it's a good idea. In fact, it's a great idea." She narrowed her eyes. "Who knew you were so romantic?"

He kissed his sister on the cheek, whispered, "Thanks," then slipped out the front door and jogged across the lawn.

Chapter 11
Faith

I should have gone.

Faith had chastised herself ever since Nate left, wondering why she hadn't gone to the party. Not because she wanted to meet new people, but because she would have been with Nate. And he obviously wanted her to go. If only she could let go of the ridiculous notion that Nate's friendship was based on ulterior motives.

An hour later, her doorbell rang. Now that she was friends with Nate, it rang more than it had the entire time she'd lived there. With a sigh, she pushed herself off the couch, went to the door, and peered out the window.

It was Nate.

Faith smoothed her hair before opening the door. He smiled at her.

"Hi," she murmured. "Wh-what are you doing here?"

"Do you want to watch a movie?" he asked.

"A movie? But what about your party?"

"Eh, I can hang out with those idiots any time. Besides, it's not really *my* party, it's my sister's party. And Mason's."

A strong, crisp breeze rattled the windows and made her shiver. Did Nate really want to give up an evening with his friends to spend time with her? She almost told him no, but something about the earnest look on his face made her decide differently. Another blast of cold air hit her, so Faith gestured for him to come in and close the door.

He walked past her into the living room, looking around for a few seconds until he found what he was looking for. He pointed at her TV remote.

"May I?" he asked.

Faith nodded.

Nate snatched up the remote, turned on the TV, and quickly flipped through her streaming services, which didn't take long since she only had a few. He sat on the edge of her couch and pulled up a movie.

She smiled when she saw what it was.

"*The Princess Bride*?" She couldn't believe that was the one he chose. It was one of her favorites; she had seen it more times than she could count.

He grinned. "Yeah. I saw the book on your kitchen table. It looked like you'd read it a lot, so I thought maybe you liked the movie, too."

"I *love* the movie," Faith replied.

"Great! Why don't you come sit by me and we'll watch it? I promise I won't bite." He winked at her, and her heart skipped a beat.

Half an hour later, they were side by side, watching the movie and eating from a bowl of popcorn balanced on the couch cushion between them. Faith shoved herself into the corner of the couch, but it wasn't big enough for her to get too far away from him. The only thing separating them was the bowl.

She concentrated on the movie, but sitting next to Nate unnerved her. He wore low-slung jeans and a tight white T-shirt, so tight it emphasized his biceps and taut abs. His fingers occasionally brushed against hers when they both reached for popcorn, and his infectious laugh echoed through the room. Faith watched him more than the movie. She couldn't help but wonder what it would be like to sit beside him with his arm around her, the two of them cuddled close together. It was easy to picture.

Unnerved by the direction her thoughts had turned, she jumped to her feet. "Would you like some hot chocolate?"

"Hot chocolate?" Nate mumbled.

"Yes," she replied. "I make fantastic hot chocolate. Trust me, you'll love it. I'll be right back."

She hurried to the kitchen and pulled ingredients from the cupboards. Every few seconds, she snuck a look at Nate. He was so relaxed, and sure of himself, sprawled over her couch like he'd been there forever, like he belonged. Meanwhile, she was a bundle of nerves, shaky and on edge. Faith envied him.

She propped herself against the counter, hugging herself as she tried to control her breathing. The hot chocolate was an excuse to get away for a few minutes so she could pull herself together. Nate probably thought she was insane or, more likely, he wondered what he had gotten himself into. Faith was willing to bet he was planning his escape.

The boiling milk interrupted her musings, drawing her attention away from her feelings of inadequacy.

The shot of Irish cream she added to the hot chocolate would calm her frazzled nerves. She prepared two mugs, topping both with a healthy dollop of whipped cream.

Nate gave her a heart-stopping smile when she reentered the room. He jumped to his feet to move a stack of books from the coffee table to the floor, making room for the popcorn bowl and both mugs. He took a mug, hissing when he touched the hot cup, and put it on the table beside the popcorn.

When they sat down, he was right next to her, his leg pressed against hers, one arm on the back of the couch, his hand close but not quite touching her. The smell of his cologne wrapped itself around her and pushed its warm scent into her nose, fogging her brain. She needed a distraction, and fast.

Faith raised her mug and sucked in a deep breath. The dark chocolate and whipped cream mixed perfectly to slice through the fog and clear her mind. She glanced at Nate out of the corner of her eye.

"Um ... Faith." He chuckled and tapped the side of his nose.

"What?"

Nate's hand landed on her leg as he leaned into her. "Here," he whispered. The pad of his thumb swiped across the tip of her nose. He held it up and showed her the whipped cream she must have gotten on her nose when she shoved her face into her drink.

Faith couldn't take her eyes off him as he pushed his thumb between his lips and sucked on it. Heat pooled in the pit of her stomach, and an indescribable need roared through every nerve ending. She opened her mouth— probably to say something stupid—but she snapped it closed as Nate moved closer. His fingers danced down her back, and he slipped his arm around her waist. His mouth was a breath away from hers. He was going to kiss her, and in that moment, there wasn't anything she wanted more than to feel his lips against hers.

The crash was loud enough to make them both jump. It ruined the moment and broke them apart. His foot had bumped the stack of books he'd put on the floor, which hit another stack of books, followed by the end table, knocking over the precariously balanced lamp and sending it crashing to the ground. It shattered into pieces.

Ten minutes later, they stood at Faith's front door. Once they cleaned up the mess and the broken glass was in the trash, Nate looked at the clock and declared it was late and he had to get up early. Faith stared at the floor and shifted from foot to foot with her lower lip caught between her teeth and her hands clenched at her sides. She wondered if he'd kiss her before he left. Actually, she hoped he'd kiss her before he left.

Instead, he grabbed her hand, gave it a quick squeeze, and mumbled something that sounded vaguely like, "I'll see you later" before he disappeared out the door.

"Bye," she whispered.

Chapter 12

Nate

As soon as the door closed behind him, Nate took off at a dead run across the lawn, like his ass was on fire. The strangest feeling had overcome him.

Doubt.

He had always gotten the girl. There had never been a question of if or when, never. Any girl he ever wanted fell head over heels for him.

Until Faith.

God, he'd wanted to kiss her when they'd stood in front of her door. He wanted to reignite the spark the broken lamp put out, but Faith stared at the floor and shifted nervously, acting like she wanted nothing more than for him to leave. She wouldn't make eye contact with him. So, he left, turned tail and ran, his confidence in his ability to win over a woman shaken.

Nate opened his front door, darted inside, and slammed it behind himself, harder than he intended.

Everyone was gone, except for Mason and Natasha, who was sprawled across the couch with her mouth open, light snores coming from her.

"Shh," Mason hissed, pointing at Natasha. "She's asleep."

"Sorry," Nate mumbled. He kicked off his shoes, went into the kitchen, grabbed a beer from the refrigerator, and drained it in a few swallows. He took out another one and dropped into a chair at the table.

Mason sat down across from him. He glanced at Natasha, leaned on the table, and said in a low voice, "What's wrong? I thought you were with the neighbor. Faith, right?"

"I was." Nate shrugged.

Mason chuckled. "Honestly, I didn't expect you home tonight. At least not at... what?" He checked his watch. "Shit, eleven-thirty. I figured you'd be staying the night."

"Faith isn't like that," Nate snapped. "She's... she's different. Hell, I'm not even sure she likes me."

"You're joking?" Mason shook his head. "None of your usual moves worked? Hard to believe."

"Believe it, buddy," Nate muttered. He leaned on the table, his head in his hands. "I can't figure her out. It's not like it usually is with a woman I'm interested in. It's not—"

"Easy?" Mason finished. He ignored the dirty look Nate gave him. "You know what, Nathaniel? Maybe she's not like the women you're usually interested in. In fact, I'm sure she's not. You're going to have to work for this one. But think about this: *if* you win her over, this might be the real deal. Especially for her. You need to be careful, and you need to be sure of what you're doing. Otherwise, you'll break her heart."

Nate nodded. Mason was right. Faith was different, and if he won her over, it wouldn't be like the other women he'd dated. Faith could be the *one*. His head spun with the possibilities.

"I'm gonna go to bed," he said, pushing himself away from the table. As he passed his sister on the couch, he turned back to Mason. "Are you leaving Tasha on the couch?"

"Hell, no. She's never sleeping there again." Mason jumped to his feet, bounded across the room, scooped Natasha up, and threw her over his shoulder.

"Hey," she mumbled sleepily. "What the heck?"

Nate laughed and headed for his room. Natasha had slept on the couch for months after a nasty breakup, until she and Mason finally got it together and realized they were in love. As much as he joked about how *icky* they were, Nate appreciated his sister finding love with his best friend. They were perfect for each other and meant to be a couple.

Once he was in his room, he peeled off his clothes and dropped onto the bed. He actually had to get up early, that's why he called it a night. Cecily Devereaux was coming to the bar in the morning to discuss his expansion plans for the Time Out Bar & Grill. If she liked what she saw, he was going to ask her to invest in the business. Nate had been working on this for months, though he had kept it to himself. Expanding the bar was a dream he hadn't thought possible until Cecily expressed an interest in his expansion plans. She was a sharp businesswoman, in charge of a multi-million-dollar company, and if he wanted to convince her to give him a lot of money, he needed to be on top of his game.

Instead of falling asleep, he stared at the ceiling, thinking about Faith, going over every move, word, and little thing he had done. Nate made himself crazy figuring out what he did to make her uncomfortable.

He couldn't get her out of his head—her soft skin, her sweet voice, and how insanely beautiful she was, though she didn't seem to know it. When he closed his eyes, all he saw was her, and all he thought about was how her lips would feel moving against his.

"Screw it," he muttered under his breath. He tossed the blankets aside, grabbed a pair of sweats and a T-shirt off the floor, and yanked them on. He threw open his door, stalked through the house, slipped on the old tennis shoes he kept by the door, and went out his front door. Nate ran across the lawn and up her porch steps. Without hesitating, he pounded on her door, not relenting until she opened it.

Faith's hair hung down her back, and she wore a baggy T-shirt, oversized boxers, and thick, wool socks pulled up to her knees. He saw more of her than he'd ever seen before, fanning the flames of his desire. She squinted at him, her eyebrows drawn together, her mouth in a tight, irritated line.

"Nate? What the heck?"

It was the only thing he let her get out before he crossed the threshold and grabbed her, his hands on her face, cupping her cheeks. He kissed her gently, his lips moving against hers.

Faith gasped and put her hands on his wrist, but she didn't resist, didn't pull away. In fact, she leaned into him, and her mouth opened. His tongue slipped into her mouth. God, she tasted like hot chocolate.

He groaned as he wrapped an arm around her waist, pulling her flush against him. Her hands slipped hesitantly around his neck, and her fingers slid up into his hair as the kiss deepened.

When they broke apart, they were both breathing heavily and staring into each other's eyes.

"That's how I should have said good night," Nate murmured.

—

After kissing Faith two more times, Nate returned to his place, crawled into bed, and slept better than he'd slept in weeks. Not even the worry about his upcoming meeting with Cecily could kill his good mood. He woke up with a smile on his face, and it stayed there. He grinned at the barista who made his coffee, grinned at the guy taking forever to cross the street and making him late, and smiled at Brooke when he walked into the bar.

"What's with you?" Brooke asked.

Nate shrugged one shoulder. "I'm just in a good mood."

"Okay," Brooke said, drawing out the word. "Why?"

"Because I am," he muttered, rolling his eyes.

"There's something you're not telling me." She stared at him until he wanted to squirm. He refused to let her ruin his good mood, though.

"Yep," he replied, smirking. He poured himself a cup of coffee from the pot behind the counter. "Don't bother digging for information because you're not getting it."

"Fine." Brooke crossed her arms. "Are you ready for this? Cecily will be here any minute."

Brooke was the only person who knew about his plan to expand the bar. She'd helped him put together a business plan to present to Cecily, even sketching the way the bar would look with the expansion. She cared almost as much as he did.

"I'm going to run upstairs and make a phone call," he said. He drank the rest of his coffee and put the cup in the small sink.

"Did you not hear me when I said Cecily is going to be here any minute?"

"Yes, I heard you," he mumbled. "Fine, I'll wait. You know what? I think I need more coffee."

As he poured himself a cup from the pot behind the counter, Cecily breezed in, her husband, Lincoln, and their dogs in tow. Nate shook both Cecily's and Lincoln's hands, then petted both dogs. Whenever Cecily came in, she had her Shih Tzu, Sebastian, with her. He was the inspiration for the pet area Nate planned to build at the back of the bar, including covered seating and a small play yard for the dogs.

Cecily Devereaux was Lakeside's resident "rich girl." She lived in an immense house on an island in the middle of Flathead Lake with Lincoln and their dogs. While she wasn't originally from Montana, she had adopted the town as her own after moving there when she was a teenager. She'd been receptive to Nate's ideas about expanding the Time Out Bar & Grill because she loved Lakeside and wanted to be a part of making it a vacation destination.

Once everyone had coffee and the doughnuts Brooke brought, Nate laid out his plans for expanding the bar. Cecily was all business, asking questions and jotting notes in a small notebook she'd pulled from her purse.

Occasionally, Brooke interjected an important piece of information or pointed out something on her drawings.

"This looks amazing," Cecily said when Nate finished speaking. "Your sketches are fabulous, Brooke."

She grinned. "Thank you."

"So, what do you think?" Nate asked.

"This is a brilliant plan," Cecily replied. "If you don't mind, I'd like a few days to go over everything."

Nate nodded. "Absolutely."

"Great." Cecily got to her feet and ordered Sebastian and their other dog, Sadie, to her side. They immediately obeyed. Lincoln attached their leashes while Cecily gathered everything and put it in her bag.

After everyone left, Nate went upstairs to his office, dropped into his chair, and grabbed the phone. He dialed Faith's number from memory. She answered on the first ring.

"H-hello?"

"Hi," he breathed. "How are you?"

"I'm okay," she replied. "You?"

"I'll be better if you say yes to a date tomorrow."

Faith laughed, an enticing, breathy laugh that made Nate's stomach twist oddly.

"Does that mean yes?" he asked.

"Yeah. I mean, yes. Yes, I'll go on a date with you tomorrow."

Nate exhaled. He'd been holding his breath, waiting for her answer, sure her it would be no. Now that she'd agreed to go, he could relax. He knew exactly what they were going to do. He needed to make a phone call.

Chapter 13

Faith

When she woke up the next morning, she'd convinced herself that Nate kissing her senseless at her front door while she was in her pajamas couldn't possibly be real. Then he called her, and before she knew what happened, she had agreed to go on a date with him. A date meant going out in public, and the thought terrified her. How was this her life?

She texted him several times in a thinly veiled attempt to get him to tell her where they were going. He didn't fall for it, keeping her guessing.

Late Sunday afternoon, Nate knocked on her door. She took a deep breath and willed her hands to stop shaking as she unlocked it.

"Hi." Nate's smile blinded her. He leaned against her door frame, calm and casual, incredibly handsome in a pair of jeans and a dark green button-down shirt. He straightened and held his hand out to her.

"Shall we?"

Faith nodded and took his hand. This was it, the *date*. She still couldn't believe she was going out with Nate, or that she'd kissed him, or that he wanted to spend time with her. She didn't understand what he saw in her.

As usual, Nate opened the passenger side door and helped her into the truck. Despite her repeated protests over the last week, he *always* opened her door and helped her in and out of the truck. He said his mom would "beat his ass" if he wasn't a gentleman.

They drove down U.S. 93, turned right on Adams, and parked in the lot by Volunteer Park. He jogged around the front of the vehicle and helped her out, then he tucked her hand into the crook of his elbow and kissed her temple.

Heat rushed to her cheeks. She could get used to this.

"Where are we going?" she asked.

"I wanted to show you something," he said. "I think you'll like it."

They crossed the street, then Nate stopped in front of a small storefront at the corner of the building. "Here we are." He pointed at the sign on the building.

Faith stepped back to read it. "Turn the Page," she mumbled. "What is this?" She eyed him suspiciously.

"Come on. I'll show you." Nate opened the door and gestured for her to go inside.

When she stepped across the threshold, the smell of new books assaulted her. She froze, astonished at what was in front of her. It was a large space, unbelievably so, considering the size of the storefront. Overflowing bookshelves crowded every available inch, signs pointed to every imaginable genre, and stacks of books covered the tables placed in various locations, their themes placed on signs prominently displayed in the center of the table. At the back of the store, a wrought iron staircase spiraled up to another level.

Faith's jaw dropped as she turned to look at Nate. "I didn't know there was a bookstore in Lakeside."

He raised his eyebrows. "Surprise!" He chuckled. "I thought you might like it." He looked around, then yelled, "Vera!"

A pretty brunette came around the corner and made her way toward them. She was ethereal, gorgeous, and when she hugged Nate, a surge of jealousy and intense inadequacy washed over Faith.

"Faith, this is my friend, Vera. She owns this place. Its grand opening is in two weeks, right?"

Vera turned her brilliant smile on Faith. She grasped Faith's hand and said warmly, "It's nice to finally meet you." She looked over her shoulder and yelled, "Oscar! Come meet Nate's girlfriend."

Faith's heart skipped at the word "girlfriend." Was that who Vera thought she was? Should she correct her? After all, she *wasn't* Nate's girlfriend; they were friends, nothing more. She sneaked a glance at Nate, but he seemed nonplussed at the comment.

A short, stocky man appeared from the stacks, carrying several boxes. He set them on the floor, dusted off his hands, and joined them. He slipped his arm around Vera's waist.

"Oscar, this is Faith," Vera said.

"Nice to meet you," he said.

She smiled shyly. "It's nice to meet both of you."

Vera's smile was so warm and inviting it instantly put Faith at ease. "I understand you're a book lover?"

She nodded. "I guess I am. I'm a librarian at the town library."

"That's why you look familiar." Vera laughed. "I love the library! I spent countless hours there during college. Well, come on. I'll show you around."

"O-okay," Faith stammered. She looked at Nate, and he gestured for her to follow Vera.

For the next two hours, Faith followed Vera around while Nate trudged after them, laughing at her obvious delight when she discovered something new. He carried her books and even got her and Vera coffee from a small coffee bar at the back of the store.

When they emerged from the bookstore, Nate carried two overstuffed bags of books tucked under his arms, and Faith couldn't stop smiling and giggling. Vera insisted Faith return for the grand opening as she and Oscar waved goodbye from the door. She readily agreed.

Giddy with excitement, Faith bounced on the balls of her feet and talked nonstop about the bookstore and everything she had experienced. She had fallen in love with Turn the Page, and she couldn't wait to return. When they got to his truck, he set the bags on the ground and pulled her into his arms.

"Did you have fun?" he asked.

"Yes! It was amazing. Thank you!" Her heart pounded and her cheeks were hot. How had her life changed so much in such a short time?

Nate kissed the corner of her mouth. "You're welcome," he whispered. He scooped up the bags and put them in the truck. "Let's go get some food. Lugging around those books made me hungry."

Once they were in the truck, on impulse, Faith reached over and took Nate's hand. His eyebrows shot up, but he quickly recovered, replacing his look of surprise with a smile. He drove with one hand while holding Faith's hand tightly with the other.

—

At work on Monday, Faith couldn't stop talking about Vera's bookstore. She went on and on about every little corner of it until Caroline interrupted her.

"Wait a minute. How did you get into the store before it opened? I thought it didn't open until next month?"

She shrugged. "Nate went with me."

Caroline stopped dead in her tracks and turned around to look at Faith. "*Nate*? The same Nate who owns the Time Out Bar & Grill?"

Faith nodded.

"Why did he take you?" Caroline asked.

"Um... well, he, uh, he knows the owner. They're friends," Faith explained.

Caroline narrowed her eyes. "That doesn't explain why he took you there before it opens."

"We're friends," she whispered.

"You're friends with Nate? Since when?"

Faith exhaled loudly, blowing her hair off her forehead. "He ran into me one night in my front yard. The next thing I know, he's asking me out for coffee."

"What? When? Why didn't you tell me?" Caroline actually looked hurt.

"I'm sorry," Faith murmured. "It's just... well, I didn't want to go out with him."

Caroline's eyes widened. "Why didn't you want to go out with him? He's attractive, funny, owns his own business—"

"I know all that," Faith said. "I guess, um, I thought he felt bad for running into me. But then he helped me when my car broke down. He did this really cute thing with a bunch of different drinks from The Percolator, and he watched *The Princess Bride* with me. His idea. He finally won me over, so I went out with him."

"Are you going out with him again?"

Faith nodded, heat rushing to her cheeks. "I want to. I really like him, and I had so much fun at the bookstore." Her eyes dropped to the floor. "Life experience has taught me that the people I care about end up hurting me. I don't want that to happen with Nate." Tears welled up in her eyes. She brushed them away, but she didn't look up. She couldn't stand the thought of Caroline looking at her with pity.

Caroline hugged her, taking Faith by surprise.

"What was that for?" she murmured.

Her friend shrugged. "Just because." She cleared her throat. "Why don't we get some work done? Tell me more about the bookstore while we shelve the new books. Let's put some flyers up around the library to get the word out."

"Yeah, that sounds great," Faith said. "I'll see if Nate can ask Vera if she has any."

She followed Caroline down the hall. Her friend was being too nice. It hadn't been hard to recognize her hug for what it really was: sympathy. Faith had grown used to things like that growing up in foster care. She didn't want people feeling sorry for her. That was her biggest fear with Nate: that it was a front because he thought she was pathetic, or he pitied her. She couldn't bear it if that was the case.

Chapter 14

Nate

Three weeks.

Nate had been dating Faith for more than three weeks, and somehow, he'd kept things quiet and low-key.

Since their first date, they had spent a lot of time together. Not only was he driving her to work every day, but they'd gotten pizza at Roselli's, she'd made homemade macaroni and cheese for dinner, he'd hung out at her place and watched a football game while she read a book, and one Friday night he fell asleep on her couch after working at the bar. They'd exchanged hellos, and then he'd rested his head on the back of the couch, closed his eyes, and the next thing he knew, he was out. Faith had thrown a blanket over him, and when he woke a couple of hours later, she'd been sitting on the floor reading.

It was the best thing to happen to him in years, and he was terrified he was going to mess it up.

"When do we get to meet the mysterious woman next door who captured the heart of our resident ladies' man?" Natasha asked.

Nate glared at his sister, willing her to shut up. He didn't want to explain his relationship with Faith to his friends.

He chuckled and shook his head. "Never. You'll scare her away." He might have laughed, but he certainly wasn't joking. His core group of friends—his sister, Mason, Oscar, Gavin, Vera, and Summer—were a raucous bunch. Loud, crazy, and fun-loving. Faith was shy, quiet, and kept to herself. She wasn't used to being around a group of people like his friends.

"Vera and Oscar got to meet her," Mason argued.

"Vera isn't loud and scary," Nate retorted. "Or sarcastic and sassy." He looked pointedly at Natasha.

His sister stuck her tongue out at him as she poured herself another beer. They were at the bar, eating Nate's food and drinking his beer after spending the day moving Mason and Natasha's things into their new place.

"What about Oscar? He's loud and scary," Natasha quipped.

Nate sighed. "He behaved himself because Vera told him if he didn't, she'd kick his ass."

"Seriously, when do we get to meet her?" Summer asked.

"She's really shy." Nate rubbed his forehead. "I don't want to scare her away. I promise you'll get to meet her. Eventually."

"Doesn't she live next door to you? Next time we're over at your place, let's walk over and say hi," Gavin interjected.

Nate glared at his friend. "I will kill you," he warned. "Don't you dare go over there."

Gavin laughed. "Okay, okay. This is serious, isn't it? You really like this woman."

He nodded. "Yeah, I do." He liked her more than any of his friends—except maybe Mason—realized.

Summer leaned on the table and stared at Nate, her eyes boring into him. "Have you slept with her?" she asked.

"Whoa, Summer," Natasha yelled. "TMI!"

"It's a legitimate question," Summer said. "Look, we know Nate is a ladies' man. We've seen the women he's paraded in and out of his place. None of those 'relationships' lasted more than what—a few weeks, maybe a month? The common denominator in all of those encounters was they started out in the same place. The bedroom. So, again, it's a legitimate question. Are you having sex with her?"

The group groaned collectively, acting appalled that Summer was asking these questions. Except Nate suspected they wanted the answers.

"No, no, wait." He raised his voice to be heard over his friends. "It's okay." He cleared his throat. "Look, not that it's anybody's business, but no, I am not having sex with Faith, even though we've been dating for three weeks." He took a deep breath. "That's not... I'm not in this to get laid. I genuinely like this woman. I'm not rushing into anything."

Everyone was shockingly quiet, staring at him like he'd grown another head. Mason smirked. His sister had a sappy smile on her face, and everyone else looked shocked.

Nate wasn't surprised; it shocked him as well. Faith had wormed her way into his heart like no other woman ever had. He hadn't felt this way since Elle. And somehow he'd messed that up. He had no intention of doing that again.

"Well, now I've heard everything," Gavin muttered. "I think I need more beer." He grabbed the pitcher and filled his glass.

Soon, the conversation moved on to other things, things that fortunately were not his love life. It was a relief because he didn't enjoy having it scrutinized.

He glanced at his watch, wondering if he could escape from his friends, take some food over to Faith's place, and hang out with her for a while. He grabbed his phone to text her.

[Nate: I might get away early. Do you want me to bring dinner over?]

[Faith: Sorry, but I'm working late. The librarian who works the evening shift is sick.]

[Nate: Okay. Can I come over when you get home?]

[Faith: Yes. I'll be there by 9:30.]

Nate shoved his phone in his pocket and refilled his beer. He still wasn't sure where he stood with Faith. He liked her and he thought she liked him, but it wasn't like it had been with other women. Those had been easy; those women had let him know from the onset they were interested and *wanted* to have sex with him. Faith was an enigma. While he thought she enjoyed his company, sometimes it was like pulling teeth to get her to go out on a date with him. Even though he'd told his friends they hadn't met Faith because they'd scare her away, the truth was she resisted every time he suggested meeting them.

And sex, well, he didn't know where they were on that subject. Not that he wasn't interested in sex with Faith, but there was something holding her back. Because he liked her so much, he had no intention of pushing her into anything she didn't want to do.

Two hours later, everyone was gone except Mason and Natasha. He sat at the table with them, nursing his beer, his thoughts constantly turning to Faith. He was antsy, checking his watch every few minutes, counting the minutes until he could see her.

Natasha rapped her knuckles on the table. "What is up with you? I've never seen you like this."

"Neither have I," Mason added. "You're not acting like yourself."

"I'm fine," Nate scoffed. "I'm... I don't know—"

"In love?" his twin asked.

"No," he muttered. "I'm... I'm not in love."

Natasha patted his arm. "You know what? You deserve love. You've been alone for too long. I worry about you."

"I'm *fine*," Nate repeated.

"I know you're fine," Natasha said. "But you're better with Faith in your life. You are aware of that, right?"

He nodded, then checked his watch. "I need to go. I want to take a shower before Faith gets home from work." He pushed his beer away and stood up.

"Are you okay to drive?" Mason asked.

"I drank half a beer," he replied, pointing at his glass. "I've been nursing it for hours." He kissed his sister on the top of the head and slapped Mason's shoulder. "Have fun in your new place. I'll see you later."

"Don't do anything I wouldn't do," Mason yelled after him.

"I hate you guys," he yelled over his shoulder as he walked away.

Once he was in his truck, Nate rolled his window down. It was cold outside, especially now that it was moving into November. But he needed the cool air to clear his head. His sister filled it with all kinds of ideas, things he didn't want to think about. He wasn't in love; he couldn't be. He'd only known Faith for about a month, not long enough to fall in love with her.

Besides, it wasn't love. He wasn't good at love. Elle had let him know that in no uncertain terms. She'd been clear when she broke up with him that he was a selfish, no-good piece of shit who didn't know how to love anybody but himself. So how could he possibly be in love with Faith?

Chapter 15

Faith

*H*er life was crazy. Crazy in a good way.

If someone told her six months ago that she would be in a whirlwind romance, the kind she'd only read about in romance novels—the insta-love, no slow burn kind of romance—Faith would have said they were crazy. Most days, it was like a dream and didn't seem real.

She'd had been dating Nate for almost a month. They spent most of their free time together, doing everything from dinner dates in Kalispell to watching TV. Well, he watched TV while she read a book.

Nate drove her to work every morning and picked her up every night until the mechanic finished fixing her car. Even if he wasn't opening the bar, he got out of bed and drove her to work, and he took a break to pick her up if he was at work.

Once she worked out an acceptable payment plan with Kane, it had still taken a couple of weeks for him to fix her car. The part he needed had to be ordered, and he had to go to Missoula to pick it up. When he'd messaged her it was ready, she was surprised at the disappointment that rushed through her. She'd gotten used to spending that time with Nate every day, and now it was over. When she'd texted Nate to ask him if he'd take her to pick it up, he'd responded with a sad face emoji, which made her laugh.

Faith convinced herself that since she had her car back, she wouldn't see as much of Nate as she had when it was in the shop. She was wrong.

When he dropped her off at the auto shop, he'd smirked at her and said, "Don't think because Kane fixed your car that it gets you out of spending time with me." Then he'd kissed her until she thought her heart might pound out of her chest.

Every day, it astonished her he wanted to be with her. She expected him to change his mind at any minute, realize he'd made a mistake, and bail.

Faith hadn't expected to see him after she took Josie's evening shift at the library, especially since he'd spent the day helping his sister and Mason move, but he'd been at her door less than five minutes after she got home. He'd swooped in, pulled her into his arms, and kissed her.

Nate released her and followed her into the kitchen. His quiet, melancholy mood was strangely out of place. He was usually in a perpetually good mood.

"Hey, you don't have to park on the street anymore," Faith pointed out.

"Yeah," he muttered. "I guess I don't." He rocked back and forth, staring at the ground. "Anyway, I only wanted to say hi. I'm sure you're tired after working all day." He gestured at the door over his shoulder. "I'm gonna go. See you later?"

"Yeah, of course," she replied.

"Good night," he whispered. He walked out, shoulders slumped and head down.

After emptying her backpack and changing into a pair of flannel pajama pants and an oversized sweatshirt, Faith headed back to the kitchen. She couldn't get Nate off her mind. He wasn't his usual cheery self, and she wasn't sure why.

Because his sister and best friend moved out.

She stopped dead in the middle of her kitchen. Of course. Nate was alone. He and Mason had lived next door to her for years. Then Natasha moved in, filling the little house even more. But now everyone was gone, and he was alone. How could she be so stupid?

She grabbed a shopping bag from under the sink, loaded it with mugs, milk, hot chocolate mix, whipped cream, and her bottle of Irish cream liqueur, then she put on her slippers, grabbed her keys, and hurried out the door. It was cold out, colder than it had been when Nate had come over. Goosebumps rose on her skin as she darted across the lawn and knocked on his door.

For a minute, she wondered if he had gone straight to bed; she couldn't see any lights on in the house. He yanked open the door, his irritated look changing to a hesitant smile when he saw her.

"Hey," he murmured. "What are you doing here? Is everything okay?"

Faith nodded, suddenly unsure of her impulsive decision to show up on Nate's doorstep. "I... I thought I'd make you some hot chocolate." She held up the bag and pointed at it.

His smile lit up the dark night. "That sounds amazing." He opened the door wide and gestured for her to come in.

She stepped into the front entrance. The house was like hers, though Nate's kitchen was to her left and the living room was through the foyer and around the corner. She emptied the bag, placing the things she'd brought with her on the table. Nate took a pan out of the cupboard, put it on the stove, then he sat at the table, watching her while she made the hot chocolate.

"Spoons?" she asked.

He pointed to a drawer next to the sink. When the mugs were full, and the whipped cream added, Faith handed one to him.

"Let's go sit on the couch," he said.

She followed him to the living room and sat at the opposite end of the couch from Nate. It was large, far bigger than hers, which meant there was at least two feet of space between them. They sat quietly, sipping their hot chocolate.

The house was empty, lifeless. No pictures hung on the walls, and no knick-knacks decorated the shelves. Of course, this had been the home of two bachelors before Natasha moved in, and she'd taken her things with her when she moved out today. She peeked at Nate out of the corner of her eye. He stared at the wall above the TV, silent.

"Are you okay?" Faith asked.

"Hm?"

"You don't seem like yourself," she said.

Nate gave her a half-hearted grin. "I'm sorry. Shit, this is the first time you've been in my house and I'm sitting here moping. You were nice enough to come over here and make me hot chocolate and…" He trailed off with a sigh and shook his head. "It's weird, you know? I've never lived alone. I lived at home with my parents and Tasha, obviously. While I was in college, I lived with Mason at the dorms, then here. Then my sister moved in with us. Now, they're gone and I'm by myself. Everything feels off-kilter."

Faith cleared her throat. "Don't you think you'll enjoy living on your own?"

He shrugged. "I guess I'll find out, huh?" He put his mug of hot chocolate on the coffee table and stood up. "I'll be right back." He darted into the bathroom and pushed the door closed.

She sat back and sipped her cocoa. It helped warm her a little, but it was freezing in Nate's house. She wandered back toward the kitchen, looking for the thermostat. It was in roughly the same location as hers.

No wonder she was cold; it hovered around sixty degrees. She jumped when Nate wrapped his arms around her from behind. She hadn't heard him come out of the bathroom.

"Are you cold?" he whispered in her ear.

She nodded. "A little."

He hugged her close and rested his chin on her shoulder. "Thank you for coming over. And making hot chocolate." He kissed her neck, and she relaxed against him. "Can I tell you something?"

"Sure." Faith closed her eyes, wondering what he was going to say. It scared her a little.

"I'm so glad I ran into you and knocked your books out of your hand. It was the best thing to happen to me in a really long time."

"Nate," she murmured. "You're crazy."

"Crazy for you." He chuckled. "And I like it."

Faith turned in his arms and rested her hands on his chest. "I like it, too. And if you're crazy, so am I." She closed her eyes, because she couldn't look at him. "Did you know before you burst into my life like the crazy ball of energy you are, I hadn't dated anybody since high school?"

"You're kidding."

She shook her head. "No, I'm dead serious. I had an unpleasant experience with a guy in high school, and it kind of scared me off dating. Apparently forever."

"What happened?"

Faith sighed. "Do you really want to hear this story?"

"Only if you want to tell me," Nate replied.

She closed her eyes. To her surprise, she did. "Can we sit down?"

"Sure." Nate led her to the couch and sat down beside her, his big, warm hand wrapped around hers.

"Okay," she murmured. "When I was in high school, I had a friend—if you could call her that—who set me up with this guy I had a crush on. I thought he liked me, you know? It turns out, this so-called friend told him I was easy, so he only dated me for sex. We had a public break up where I came off looking like a fool *and* a bitch. I haven't dated since. And since I'm being honest about my past, I haven't kissed a guy in nine years, and I'm a virgin." She threw herself against the back of the couch and put her hands over her face.

"Hey," Nate said. He grabbed her hands and pried them away from her face. "Faith, would you look at me, please?"

She looked up at him. As soon as she did, he leaned over and kissed her. "I'm sorry people suck. That guy sounds like a jerk."

"Yeah, he was." She stared at her hands folded in her lap, caught her lower lip between her teeth, and gnawed at it.

Nate ducked his head, forcing her to look at him. "What's wrong?"

Faith shrugged one shoulder. "Does it... does it bother you that I'm a virgin?"

He shook his head. "No, of course not. Why would it bother me?"

She snorted. "Um, maybe because you usually date women who are far more experienced than me? Or, I don't know, because *you're* more experienced than me. I'm a twenty-six-year-old virgin, and you, well, you've slept with every woman in town."

Nate rolled his eyes. "You know, I'm getting really tired of everyone saying that. I don't care that you're a virgin. I'm fine if you want to have sex or if you don't want to have sex. That's not what matters to me."

"Would you be mad if I didn't want to have sex?" she whispered. "Because I'm not sure I'm ready yet."

"Absolutely not," he replied. "I'll wait as long as you want. Forever, if you want me to."

Faith blushed. "Really?"

"Yes, really." He pulled her into his arms and hugged her close.

She closed her eyes and rested her head against his chest. God, she wanted to believe him; she really did. He seemed sincere, but she couldn't seem to push away the little niggle of doubt invading her thoughts.

What if he's lying to make me feel better?

Chapter 16

Faith

The next morning, Faith was still thinking about her conversation with Nate. Keeping the tears at bay had been almost impossible. Despite his assurances to the contrary, she had convinced herself he wasn't being honest. He probably wanted to spare her feelings, which is why he said he didn't care she was a virgin. Of course he cared. He was a man. It had to bother him.

After he walked her back to her place and kissed her good night, she'd gone to bed, but she hadn't been able to sleep. Her brain wouldn't let her.

Sunday, she was on her own because Nate worked a double shift at the bar. She cleaned the house and organized her books, which didn't go exactly as planned, but she put several boxes of them in her extra bedroom.

Monday came and went without a call from Nate. She'd looked out the window several times, but his truck was nowhere to be seen. She texted him, but she didn't get an answer.

Tuesday, he showed up at the library with lunch, which made Caroline grin like she'd won the lottery.

Nate laughed as he and Faith sat down in the breakroom. "Your friend is funny. Is she happy to see me?"

She giggled. "She's just surprised. So am I. What's up?"

"Can't I come have lunch with you?" he asked.

"Yes!" she insisted, blushing. "Of course."

"I admit, I have an ulterior motive," Nate said. He reached across the table and took her hand. "I've got this big ... thing coming up. A project I'm working on. I'm afraid it's going to take up a lot of my time the next few weeks, so I won't be around much."

"Oh, um, okay," she whispered.

Was this the breakup she'd been expecting?

He squeezed her hand. "Hey, look at me. This changes nothing."

Faith nodded. "Sure, I understand."

Nate was correct; she didn't see him much over the next few weeks. She missed him terribly, and even though he swore it was this mysterious project of his, she couldn't help but wonder if this was because of what they'd discussed about sex and her virginity. She threw herself into work, staying late, doing whatever odd jobs Caroline needed done.

When she finally got a free night at home, Nate was once again working, so she organized the boxes of books she had stacked in the extra bedroom. She separated them into twenty piles, divided by genre and alphabetized. She ran out of steam when she found a box of old romance books she'd brought home a few weeks earlier. Faith had never been much of a romance reader, but curiosity got the best of her. She sorted through them until she found one that looked interesting. The next thing she knew, she'd read more than a hundred pages.

The book was racy and unbelievably sexy. As she read it, her imagination ran wild, and she couldn't help but picture Nate as the novel's main character. Images of him doing the things the guy in the book was doing to the female lead filled her head.

Headlights splashing across the window interrupted her. This room faced Nate's house, and the window overlooked his driveway. She jumped to her feet, tucked a receipt in her book to hold her place, then she went to the window. To her surprise, she saw Nate getting out of his truck. He'd told her he had to close, which meant he didn't get home until one or two in the morning, sometimes later. Instead of going inside, he ran around the front of the truck and opened the passenger side door. Hands appeared with a plastic bag of what looked like food containers from the bar. Nate took the bag, then a woman jumped out of the truck, slung a large tote bag over her shoulder, and followed him to his front door. Just before the door closed behind them, Nate glanced over his shoulder at her place.

A deep pain settled in the center of her chest, and her breath caught in her throat. She snatched her cell phone off the floor and dialed Nate's number. It rang once, then went to voicemail. A few seconds later, a text popped up.

[Nate: Busy working. Can't talk. Call you tomorrow.]

Faith's grip on her phone loosened, and it fell to the floor. He lied to her. He wasn't at work. He was home and with another woman who looked like she was prepared to stay the night. She leaned against the wall, trying to catch her breath, but after a minute, all she could do was slide to the floor, put her head on her knees, and let the tears fall.

———

After a restless night spent tossing and turning, Faith finally fell asleep around five a.m. When her alarm went off, she grabbed her phone to shut it off, then she texted Caroline to tell her she wouldn't be in. She felt stupid calling out of work because of a *man*, but her heart was in a million pieces. There was no way she could focus enough to get anything done. Not that she told Caroline it was because of Nate; she claimed she had the stomach flu.

Then she shut off her phone, pulled the pillow over her head, and to her surprise, fell asleep. She didn't wake until a few minutes before noon. Her jaw ached from clenching her teeth, a pain that radiated into her head. She turned her phone back on and found not only a sympathetic message from Caroline offering to bring her 7-Up and crackers, but multiple missed calls and texts from Nate. Those she ignored.

Faith was about to text Caroline when her phone rang in her hand with a call from her friend.

"Hey, Caroline," she answered.

"You're not sick."

"Um, what?"

"Don't um, what me," Caroline snapped. "What happened? Is something going on with Nate? He called here and did not know you were sick. Which is weird, don't you think?"

"No," Faith mumbled.

"Did you break up with him?" Caroline asked.

"I don't want to talk about it," she whispered. "It's... he's... Nate's all wrong for me."

Caroline huffed. "I'm going to give you some advice, whether or not you want it. I think you're making a mistake. A huge mistake. Has it ever occurred to you that Nate is the right kind of wrong?"

"What does that even mean?"

"On the surface, you can try to justify that Nate is wrong for you, but you know damn well he's not," Caroline explained. "He is right for you, and you know it. Don't throw what you've got with him away."

"It's too late," Faith whispered. "Look, I have to go." She hung up without waiting for a response.

Her storybook romance with Nate really had been too good to be true. He probably got tired of not having sex and found someone who would give it to him without the emotional attachment. Faith wondered if he planned to break up with her or if he thought he could keep seeing her while he slept around with other women. The more she thought about it, the angrier she got.

It took her a few minutes to drag herself out of bed, but she was finally able to get up, use the bathroom, and brush her teeth. In the kitchen, she filled the coffeepot with water and shoved a filter in it, but when she opened the tin where she kept her coffee, it was empty. Tears sprang to her eyes.

"Dammit," she muttered under her breath. "Dammit, dammit, dammit." She slammed the container down on the counter, scaring Heathcliff and sending him scurrying out of the room, most likely to hide under her bed.

She couldn't survive without coffee, not today, so she hurriedly put on her shoes, coat, gloves, and hat, grabbed her keys, and went out to her car. She glanced at Nate's house as she walked across the lawn. His truck was gone. It made her irrationally angry.

A light snow fell as she drove to The Percolator. It was beautiful, and it enraged her. She wanted the world to be ugly and horrid. Beauty had no place in a world that stole her only joy.

Her mood didn't improve when she got to the coffee shop. The line was incredibly long, so long she almost turned around and left, but she was desperate for a cup of coffee. She craved it, so she slipped in line, but kept her head down, staring at the floor, her hands shoved in her pockets.

A few minutes after getting in line, she glimpsed Nate's friend Oscar sitting at a table with another man who looked vaguely familiar. Faith didn't look up or make eye contact with Oscar, and she turned her body and pulled her hat down so he couldn't see her face. She prayed he didn't recognize her as the line moved and she got closer to their table.

"What time did Nate say to be at the bar tonight?" the man with Oscar said.

Her ears perked up at the sound of Nate's name. She squinted at the two men, pushed her glasses up her nose, and scrutinized the one she didn't know. She was pretty sure she'd seen him coming and going from the house next door in the last few years. Faith had met none of Nate's friends, aside from Vera and Oscar. Any time he suggested they get together with his friends or the people at the bar, she'd come up with an excuse not to go because she'd been too nervous to entertain the thought of meeting such important people in his life.

"Gavin!" the barista yelled, and the man with Oscar jumped to his feet, grabbed the coffee, and returned to his seat.

"How do you think he convinced her to say yes?" Gavin asked as he sat back down.

Faith's head shot up; then she quickly looked down and concentrated on what they were saying.

Oscar shrugged. "Who knows? I'm sure he charmed her in that way he has."

"Yeah, that's easy for Nate." Gavin chuckled and shook his head. "All he has to do is flash those baby blues at a woman, and she's falling over herself to give him what he wants. I didn't think he'd win her over, though. She's a tough nut to crack."

"From what Mason said, this has been in the works for a while," Oscar said. "He's been after her for some time, but he stayed quiet about it. Now that she said yes, he's ready to celebrate."

"Is she going to be there?" Gavin asked.

Oscar nodded. "Probably. I bet she's going to be around a lot now that this is a done deal."

Gavin laughed. "I wonder how Nate feels about that?"

"He loves it." Oscar snorted. "You know how he is." He checked his watch. "Hey, we better go. I'll be late. Vera has a bunch of work for me to do before opening day."

Faith inched away from the table, careful to keep her face turned away from Oscar. Not only did she not want him to know she'd been eavesdropping, she didn't want him to see the fresh tears on her cheeks. She waited until

Oscar and Gavin were gone, then she wiped her cheeks with her gloved hands.

She ordered her coffee when it was her turn, forcing herself not to run once she had it in hand. Home was a million miles away. It surprised her when she parked in front of her house because she had no memory of the drive from the coffee shop. Her brain had shut down.

Once again, she looked over at Nate's place as she crossed the lawn. She couldn't believe she'd let herself fall for such a jerk, especially one who lived right next door. He'd only been biding his time with her until he got the woman he really wanted.

As she stepped through her front door, her phone pinged with a message. When she saw it was Nate, she deleted it without reading it, then she shut off her phone.

Maybe it was time to move.

Chapter 17

Nate

Nate shoved his phone back in his pocket. Faith wasn't answering her phone or any of his text messages. He'd been calling her off and on all morning.

It was still dark when he'd left the house to head to the bar for a seven a.m. meeting with Cecily. Her flight to New York was leaving Kalispell at nine, and she wanted to meet before she and Lincoln left. Nate and Brooke had worked until three in the morning, putting the final touches on everything they had for Cecily. Brooke had crashed on his couch, and they went back to the bar together.

Cecily breezed through the front door of the bar, her Shih Tzus—Sebastian and Sadie—decked out in matching sweaters and leading the way. It took less than an hour for Cecily to go through the paperwork. She'd dragged Lincoln to a back corner of the bar, where they conversed for about ten minutes. When they returned to the table, Cecily pulled a stack of papers from her bag, signed the bottom of one with a flourish, and pushed it across the table.

"I love it," she said. "All of it." She pointed at the paper. "Consider that an open checkbook. Whatever you need for the expansion, it's yours. Go through the paperwork, and when me and Lincoln get back from New York, we'll meet. But it's a yes."

Nate shot out of his seat with a shout, startling the dogs. He hugged Cecily and shook Lincoln's hand, then he grabbed Brooke and hugged her until she begged him to let her go.

An hour after she entered the bar, Cecily was gone.

The first person Nate called was Faith, but it went straight to voicemail. He texted her and asked her to call him as soon as she could.

After that, he called his sister and Mason, as well as all their friends. It was a relief to let the cat out of the bag and tell everyone what he and Brooke had been up to for the last few weeks. He made them all promise to join him at the bar for a celebration that night.

Once he'd talked to his friends, he tried Faith again. Straight to voicemail. Maybe she broke her phone. That thought prompted him to look up the library's number.

"Lakeside College Library, this is Caroline. How may I help you?"

Nate cleared his throat. "Um, hi, Caroline. This is Nate Garin. I'm a friend of Faith's. Can I speak to her?"

"Oh, Nate, hi. Uh, she's not here. Faith called in sick this morning."

"Sick?"

"Yeah, she said she had the stomach flu," Caroline said.

"Thanks." He hung up and immediately texted Faith.

[Nate: I'm worried about you. Call me, please.]

He tried not to worry about Faith as he made preparations for the evening's celebrations, but it wasn't easy. His mind kept drifting to her. Around three, he slipped into the back room and called her again.

"Hello?" She sounded odd, almost unsure of herself.

"Hey, I've been calling you," he said. "Are you okay?"

She took a deep breath. "Can you please stop calling me? I don't want to talk to you."

"What?"

"Don't call me. Don't text me. I don't want to talk to you."

"What the hell are you talking about?" he snapped.

"I'm glad I know the truth now."

"The truth? The truth about what? Jesus, Faith, are you crying? Tell me what's wrong. What happened?"

She laughed, a horrible, sad sound that made his heart ache. "You know what? I should have known better. I was stupid to think you cared about me or wanted to be with me. Was I some kind of consolation prize? Someone to kill time with until you got the woman you wanted?"

Nate closed his eyes and squeezed his phone. "You're not making any sense."

"You don't have to be nice to me anymore," she whispered. "Go back to pretending I don't exist." The line disconnected.

—

After the phone call, Nate bolted, running up the back stairs to his office. He was furious, the anger and the damn feelings he'd ignored rushing up out of nowhere and overwhelming him. He sat down behind his desk and stared at the wall, which was where his sister and Mason found him. Mason set three beers on the desk and took a seat while Natasha came around and perched on the edge.

"What?" Nate mumbled.

"Tell me what's wrong," she said.

"Nothing is *wrong*," he replied.

"Bullshit. Brooke said you've been up here all afternoon, acting moody and depressed. I think she used the word mopey." Her eyes narrowed. "You didn't break up with Faith, did you?"

"No." He sighed, rested his head against the chair, and pinched the bridge of his nose. "She broke up with me."

"What? Why?" Natasha crossed her arms and glared at him. "What did you do?"

He gave his sister a dirty look. "I didn't *do* anything. The last time I saw her, everything was great. Then, out of nowhere, she told me to leave her alone. Something about her being a filler girlfriend until I got the one I wanted. I don't know what the hell she's talking about."

"Filler girlfriend? Does she think you're seeing someone else?" Natasha asked. "Wait. Are you seeing someone else?"

"Tasha, give him a break," Mason said.

Nate laid his head on his desk, his voice muffled when he spoke. "I never should have let myself get close to her. I'm so stupid. I swore I wouldn't let another woman break my heart, and then this happens. God, I'm an idiot."

"What is he talking about?" Natasha demanded. "Who broke his heart and when?"

"Elle," Mason replied.

Natasha poked him. "The girl you dated in college? I don't understand."

Nate sat up, resting his chin on his hand. "Elle and I dated for two years. More than that, I think. Anyway, I thought we were in a good place. I decided to propose."

"What?" Natasha yelled. She slapped Nate on the arm. "You were going to propose to your girlfriend, and I am just now finding out about it? I am your sister."

"A sister who was conspicuously absent when we were in college and for a couple of years after," Nate snapped.

"Sorry," she whispered. "Go on."

"Anyway, I planned on proposing to Elle, but out of nowhere, she dumped me. No actual explanation, only a lame excuse about how we'd drifted apart because all I cared about was my bar. She didn't even do it in person. She sent me a text message in the middle of the day while I was at work. Six months later, she got married."

"Oh my God, Nate." Natasha threw her arms around him and hugged him. "I'm so sorry."

"You're choking me," he mumbled.

"Sorry." She released him, grabbed a beer, and paced the length of the room. "This explains so much. You turned into a man whore because someone broke your heart. So, you decided it was easier to fuck around with a bunch of women than it was to settle down with one. Right?"

"Thanks for the analysis, Dr. Freud," Nate muttered. "Unfortunately, you're right. I was afraid to get close to anybody."

"So, that's why, if a woman wanted more, you dumped her." She took a drink of her beer and grinned triumphantly. "You're not completely broken; you were protecting yourself."

"Will you quit acting like you've solved some big mystery, please?" Nate muttered while Mason laughed and snorted.

"I would apologize," Natasha said, "but I am ecstatic that I figured out why the hell you were sleeping around. Nobody wants a man whore for a brother."

Nate rolled his eyes. "This is not helping me."

Mason, who had been surprisingly quiet, suddenly spoke up. "Are you in love with Faith?"

Nate's immediate instinct was to protest, deny that any feelings existed. He opened his mouth, then he shut it again. He couldn't say that because it would be a lie.

He loved Faith. Jesus, he wanted to spend every second of every day with her, and even that wasn't enough. This breakup and her sudden refusal to see him wounded him to his core.

"Nate?" Mason prompted. "Do you love her?"

"Yes," he whispered, afraid if he said it too loud, it would somehow ruin everything. "Yes, I love her."

"Can I make a suggestion?" Mason asked.

"Yeah, of course."

"You need to tell her how you feel," his best friend said. "Lay it all out for her. It's the only thing that will save your relationship."

"I don't know—"

"Trust me, I know what I'm talking about," Mason interjected. He glanced at Natasha. "Take it from someone who almost blew it with the woman he loves. Be honest."

"Mason is right," Natasha added. "Go talk to Faith. Tell her how you feel and fix this. Do whatever you need to do."

Nate nodded, got to his feet, and grabbed his jacket. "You're right. I can't sit here and wonder what the hell went wrong. I need to talk to her and do whatever I have to in order to convince her not to break up with me."

Chapter 18

Faith

Nothing she'd done in her life was harder than telling Nate to leave her alone—not her emancipation at sixteen, not her move from Texas to Montana, not even going through six years of college to get her master's degree. The pain in her chest, in her *heart*, was almost unbearable. When she'd told him it was over, she'd cried, despite how hard she tried not to break down. Faith let the tears fall. She needed to get it out, get Nate out of her system, and if she had to do that with bucket-loads of tears, so be it.

For the last hour, she'd been on the couch underneath her warmest blanket with Heathcliff on her lap, tormenting herself by watching *The Princess Bride* and thinking about Nate. Occasionally, she yanked a tissue out of the box on the table and wiped her eyes. Since she'd never broken up with anyone, she had no clue how long the pain was going to last. A day, a week, a month, a *year*? Time stretched endlessly out in front of her.

The pounding on her door startled both her and Heathcliff. The cat launched himself off her lap, knocking over a stack of books on his way to her bedroom. Faith got up, wrapped the blanket around herself like a protective cocoon, and went to the door. Even though she thought she knew who was out there, she closed one eye and looked through the peephole.

Nate.

"I know you're in there, Faith," he yelled. "Let me in!"

Why was he out there, screaming to be let in? He didn't have to pretend to like her anymore. She let him off the hook. She pulled the blanket tight around her and took a deep breath before she spoke.

"Go away," she yelled. Faith rested her forehead against the cold oak door. "Please, Nate, just go away." The tears threatened to fall again. She felt them building up, ready to break free.

"No," he said firmly. "I want to know what happened. I want to know why you broke up with me, why you're pushing me away?"

"Can't you accept that it's over?" she asked.

"It's not over," he snapped. "Let me in so we can talk."

"Don't you get it? I'm setting you free. You don't have to keep pretending to like me. I'll... I'll be okay. Go back to your life, to the woman you really want." She choked back a sob. "Please, go away."

There was no response, only silence. A quick look out the peephole showed her that Nate was still on the porch, leaning against the railing, arms crossed, staring at her front door.

"Dammit," she muttered under her breath. "Why is he so stubborn?" She took a deep breath, turned around, and returned to the couch. Nate couldn't stay out there forever, especially with the snow falling and the temperature dropping. He'd go away, eventually. All she had to do was wait him out.

—

Faith hadn't heard anything from outside her front door in quite a while, more than an hour. The last time she'd snuck a peek through the peephole, Nate was still on the porch, arms crossed, his eyes on the ground between his feet. Frustrated that he wouldn't give up and go home, she'd kicked the door with her stocking foot, hard enough to hurt, and so loud that Nate's head came up.

"Faith?" he'd called.

She had ducked as if he could see her, just like the first time he'd knocked on her door. She'd grumbled at herself as she returned to the living room and picked up a book. Not that she could concentrate on reading.

The second time she got up, she had no intention of letting Nate know she was checking on him. He was probably gone anyway. The sun had gone down, and the temperature had dropped drastically. It was too cold to be standing outside someone's door.

Faith tiptoed to the door and leaned carefully against it, nothing touching it but the tips of her fingers. Before she looked, she closed her eyes and took a deep breath, sending up a silent prayer he wouldn't be there. Then she looked.

Nate was gone.

Her breath caught in her throat, and her stomach churned. As much as she hated to admit it, she was disappointed he wasn't out there. He'd given up too easily. At least it confirmed how he really felt about her. She was turning away from the door when she heard a thump. She looked again, and to her surprise, Nate was climbing to his feet. He must have been sitting on the porch, leaning against the door.

He paced around the small porch, stomping his feet and shaking his arms. She could just make him out in the light cast by the streetlight. He'd been out there for two hours.

He's going to freeze to death.

"So what?" she said out loud. "Let him freeze."

"Faith?" Nate leaped at the door and attempted to look through the peephole.

She slapped a hand over her mouth. He must have heard her. Faith bent over, her hands on her knees. This was ridiculous. If she didn't tell him to leave, he'd stay out there all night. Resolve rushed through her, so she lunged at the door and yanked it open.

Nate fell face-first through the door, landing on his hands and knees. Faith shrieked and stumbled back, her feet tangling. She would have fallen if Nate hadn't jumped to his feet and grabbed her, keeping her upright. She put her hands on his chest and tried to push him away, but his grip on her arms was too tight.

"Let me go!"

"Faith, listen to me."

"Get out of my house, Nate," she retorted. "Now."

"No," he barked. "Not until you tell me what the hell is going on. I'll leave once you explain why you broke up with me. Tell me what I did wrong, and then I'll leave. But not before." He released her, shut the door, and stood in front of it. "Talk."

Faith closed her eyes. She couldn't look at him, knowing what he'd done. All she had to do was get through this moment in time. Once she told him she knew the truth, he'd leave, and it would be over. She could go back to her quiet, boring life.

"I know what you did," she whispered. She ran a hand through her hair, pushing it away from her face. "I saw you bring that woman home last night."

"What?"

"Last night, Nate. I saw a woman get out of your truck and go inside with you. I called you right after I saw her and you said you were working. You lied."

Realization dawned in his eyes. "I didn't lie. You misinterpreted—"

Faith shook her head. "No, I don't think so. Then this morning at the coffee shop, I overheard Oscar and Gavin talking about you getting some woman to say yes, that you'd been after her for a while, and now that you had her, you planned to celebrate. Obviously, you were using me to kill time and now that you've got the woman you want, you don't need me anymore. I broke up with you before you could breakup with me." A sob escaped her. "I should have known it was bullshit. Someone like you, a guy who could have any woman he wants, would never be interested in someone like me."

"Is that what you think?" he asked. "That I only dated you until... until someone better came along?"

Faith nodded, unable to speak out of fear that the sobs would break free.

"God, I suck at this, you know," he mumbled.

Faith wasn't even sure he was talking to her. He shoved off his jacket as he walked away from her, stopping in the middle of the living room and tossing the jacket on a chair. The tips of his ears and his nose were red bright red. He wrung his hands together as he paced around the room. She wanted to tell him to get out, to leave her alone, but she couldn't seem to do it.

Nate abruptly stopped and looked at her. "Do you know what? I am awful at relationships. Awful. I haven't had a serious relationship in four or five years."

"But all those women—"

"None of those women I dated meant shit to me. But I could talk to them, charm them, get them to like me. It was easy. But you, well, you are the one woman I need to talk to, and I don't know what the hell to say."

"What are you talking about?" Faith sat on the edge of the couch and put her head in her hands.

"Do you know Cecily Devereaux?" he asked.

Everyone knew Cecily Devereaux. She was the richest woman in Lakeside, as well as one of the nicest. Faith had met her at a library fundraiser last year and immediately liked her. They didn't cross paths often, but when they did, Cecily was always kind.

"Cecily is investing in the bar," he explained. "We've been meeting off and on for several weeks. My assistant manager, Brooke, has been helping me put together a new business plan and handling the designs for the expansion. Brooke came home with me last night to put the finishing touches on our last presentation. That was who you saw getting out of my truck. Brooke and I are friends, nothing more. Trust me, I am *not* Brooke's type. Not even close."

"I ... don't understand," Faith mumbled. "Why didn't you tell me?"

"I didn't tell anybody, not even my sister or my best friend. I was afraid of jinxing it. But this morning, after Cecily agreed to invest, I called everybody and told them. They're all at the bar right now, celebrating. Which is probably what you heard Oscar and Gavin talking about this morning."

Faith sighed. Had she jumped to the wrong conclusion? She pressed her thumbs against her forehead and closed her eyes.

"Faith, look at me."

When she opened her eyes, Nate had kneeled in front of her. He took her hands, sending a shiver racing through her thanks to his icy hands.

"I should have told you this a while ago, but I was scared. I'm not anymore." He swallowed, his throat moving noticeably.

"Told me what?" Faith asked.

"I love you," he whispered, as if saying it too loud would somehow negate the words. "I swear, I will never do anything to hurt you. I promise."

"Really?" she breathed.

"Yes, really." Nate curled his fingers around the back of her neck, caught her lips in his, and kissed her. It was the kind of kiss she'd read about in books; the kind of kiss that made someone believe in love. Made her believe in him.

Faith was breathless when they broke apart. She clung to Nate, afraid if she let go, she would collapse.

"So, are you still mad at me?" he asked quietly.

Faith laughed. "Maybe a little. I wish you'd told me about the expansion and the meetings with Cecily. I understand why you didn't, but if I'd known, I might not have freaked out."

"I'll tell you what," Nate said. "I promise I will never keep anything from you again, ever."

"I like that promise," she murmured.

Nate kissed her again. "Hey, do you want to come to the bar with me and celebrate? I think it's time for my friends to meet the woman I love."

Faith blushed. She loved how that sounded coming out of his mouth. She could definitely get used to being the woman Nate loved.

Epilogue

Faith

Eighteen Months Later

The hum of laughter and the clink of glasses filled the air, mingling with the loud music drifting from the corner stage. The polished wooden floors gleamed under the new lights, fresh flowers adorned every table, and the sound of children playing outside drifted through the open doors. Faith smoothed her skirt and glanced around the crowded room. Despite knowing almost everyone there, her hands shook and her heart raced.

Nate was holding court behind the newly finished bar, laughing as he poured drinks and accepted congratulations from not only his friends, but his regular customers as well. He'd rolled up his shirt sleeves, his tie was already loose, and he was in his element. A smiled tugged at Faith's lips. There was something so effortlessly charming about Nate when he was like this, doing what he loved. She envied him. Even after all this time, being around his friends made her a little nervous.

"Do you think he'll stop for a minute and let someone else take over?" a voice said at her side.

She turned to find Cecily smirking as she sipped from a champagne flute. Faith laughed, her gaze returning to Nate. "After the work he's put into this remodel, he deserves to celebrate."

"Yes, he does," Cecily agreed. "It exceeded my expectations."

Faith felt a pang of pride at what Nate had done. The remodel and expansion of the Time Out Bar & Grill had been his labor of love for the past eighteen months, a project he'd given every ounce of his energy. Now, the popular bar looked completely different. Nate bought the empty property next door and turned it into a sprawling outdoor area stretching all the way to Flathead Lake. He'd installed a small play area for children, making the bar and grill family friendly during the day. Brooke and Cecily had also designed a pet-friendly area for the town's many dogs. Cecily's Shih Tzus, Van's Belgian Malinois, Soldier, and Brooke's Border Collie, Mitchell, were out there breaking it in right now.

As if he sensed her thinking about him, Nate looked up and caught her gaze. His grin widened and he winked, then gestured for her to join him.

"Will you excuse me?" Faith asked.

Cecily squeezed her arm. "Of course. I'll talk to both of you later." She turned and disappeared into the growing crowd.

Heat rushed through Faith as she walked toward Nate, her heart racing. Even after all this time, she still felt like a teenager when he smiled at her.

As she approached, he slipped out from behind the bar to take her hand and kiss her cheek. "Are you enjoying yourself?" he whispered in her ear.

"Yes, and I see you are, too." She giggled. "You're in your element."

"Yeah, I love this stuff." He glanced around. "Do you have a minute? I need to talk to you about something."

Faith nodded. "Sure. I think I can tear myself away from the crowd for a few minutes."

Nate chuckled because he knew being around so many people made her nervous, even though she had become friends with *his* friends. He took her hand, led her through the new section of the bar, out the back door, and down to the beach. A cool breeze came off the water, but it was warm enough outside that it didn't bother her. Summers in Montana were her favorite.

They sat on one of the new benches, holding hands. Nate was more fidgety than usual, glancing over his shoulder every few seconds, knee bouncing, and fingers tapping.

"If you need to get back to the bar—" She trailed off as Nate dropped to his knees in front of her. "Wh-what are you doing?"

"You know, I had an entire speech planned, practiced it for hours. I even stood in front of the mirror and said it. I'm not great with flowery speeches or stuff like that." He took a deep breath and stared up at her with his gorgeous blue eyes. "Before you came into my life, I was walking around with my eyes closed. I couldn't see what I wanted, what was right in front of me, not until I ran into you. Literally, ran into you. You changed my life, Faith."

She shook her head. Her heart pounded dangerously fast. This wasn't happening. Things like this didn't happen to her.

Except they did. Ever since Nate came into her life, good things happened to her. He'd changed her life as well.

He reached into his pocket, pulled out a small velvet box, and opened it to reveal a stunning sapphire ring. She swallowed past the lump rising in her throat. He removed it from the box, then he took her left hand and slipped it on her middle finger. She stared at it, then slowly raised her eyes to look at him.

"Will you marry me?" he murmured.

Faith opened her mouth, but nothing came out. She took a deep breath and tried again.

"Yes," she whispered.

Nate smirked and leaned forward, tilting his head toward her. "I'm sorry. What did you say?"

"Yes!" she repeated loudly.

His smile widened, then he jumped to his feet and yelled, "She said yes!"

Cheers erupted from behind them. Faith spun around to see everyone standing outside, watching them. She blushed and put her hands over her face.

Nate sat down beside her, took hold of her hands, and pulled them away from her face. He cupped her cheeks and kissed her until she couldn't catch her breath.

"I love you," he said when they broke apart.

"Forever?" Faith asked.

"Always and forever."

She smiled and rested her forehead against their clasped hands, then she looked up at him.

"I love you, too."

Book Club Questions:

1. Faith and Nate are total opposites—introvert vs. extro-
   vert, bookworm vs. social butterfly. What do you think
   draws them together, and how do their differences
   help them grow individually?

2. Nate is known as a ladies' man at the start of the story.
   How did your perception of him change as the story
   progressed? Did he surprise you?

3. Faith has built strong emotional walls due to past dis-
   appointments. How did her relationship with Nate
   challenge those boundaries—and were there moments
   you thought she might retreat for good?

4. There's a theme of people not being what others
   expect them to be—Nate is more than a flirt, and
   Faith is stronger than she appears. How does the
   story challenge stereotypes or assumptions we make
   about others?

5. What do you think *Right Kind of Wrong* is saying about the idea of "the one"? Is love about finding someone who's your opposite, your match, or a mix of both?

6. If this book were to continue into a sequel or a companion novel set in Lakeside, which character would you want to see find love next—and why?

Author Bio

Mimi Francis is a sassy romance writer known for her steamy tales of passion that leave readers breathless. When she's not crafting the perfect happily-ever-after, you can find her sipping margaritas and binge-watching Marvel movies or the TV show Supernatural. But her true loves (after her husband, of course) are her four Shih Tzus who keep her company as she spins stories that will make your heart race and your toes curl. Get ready to fall in love with her characters and the worlds she creates.

Discover more at
4HorsemenPublications.com

10% off using HORSEMEN10